THE PHARAOH'S Secret

THE PHARAOH'S Secret

MARISSA MOSS

AMULET BOOKS
NEW YORK

Library of Congress Cataloging-in-Publication Data

Moss, Marissa.
The pharaoh's secret / by Marissa Moss.
p. cm.
Summary: When fourteen-year-old Talibah and her ten-year-old brother, Adom, visit modern-day Egypt with their historian father, they become involved in a mystery surrounding Hatshepsut, a woman pharoah, and Senenmut, the architect of her mortuary tomb, as well as their own deceased mother.
ISBN 978-0-8109-8378-6
1. Hatshepsut, Queen of Egypt—Fiction. [1. Supernatural—Fiction. 2. Time travel—Fiction. 3. Senenmut—Fiction. 4. Kings, queens, rulers, etc.—Fiction. 5. Pyramids—Egypt—Fiction. 6. Egyptian Americans—Fiction. 7. Cairo (Egypt)—Fiction. 8. Egypt—Fiction. 9. Egypt—History—Eighteenth dynasty, ca. 1570-1320 B.C.—Fiction. 10. Mystery and detective stories.] I. Title.

PZ7.M8535Phc 2009
[Fic]—dc22
2008022216

Amulet Books are available at special discounts when purchased in quantity for premiums and promotions as well as fundraising or educational use. Special editions can also be created to specification. For details, contact specialmarkets@abramsbooks.com or the address below.

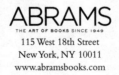

THE ART OF BOOKS SINCE 1949
115 West 18th Street
New York, NY 10011
www.abramsbooks.com

To Simon, Elias, and Asa. And to their father,
Harvey Stahl. May he find his way in the afterworld
with the Book of the Dead, and may his sons always
find their way back to him in their hearts.

Contents

The Voice

A FTER THE LONG FLIGHT I'M SO GLAD TO get out of the airplane, to move my legs again, that I forget to be excited about being here. But as we drive to the hotel, along the Nile River, a wave of wonder bubbles up inside of me. We're really here, in Cairo, and suddenly I'm wide awake. I expect to see brilliant colors and ornate palaces. Instead, I see cement slums, cardboard shanties, and then, as we get closer to the center of the city, the same anonymous buildings you see everywhere, sleek glass-and-metal high-rises next to crumbling cinder block monstrosities.

Luckily our hotel is one of the modern buildings, but I can't help feeling disappointed. This isn't how I imagined Cairo. Where are the richly woven carpets, the crowded bazaars crammed with spices, olives, and old, battered lamps that might hold a genie? I know I shouldn't expect Aladdin's adventures to come to life, but I thought Egypt would feel familiar, like a place I'd known from my dreams. Even though I was born in New York, I've always felt that once I came to Egypt, I'd recognize my real home, the place where I belong. After all, for as long as I can remember, my grandparents have been telling me stories about the country they came from, about growing up in a village south of Cairo where the wealthiest family was the one with the most camels, where there was one streetlight for the whole town—and no streets, just dirt lanes—where ancient curses and charms brought magic into the simplest lives. But this isn't an enchanted village. It's a big, ugly, modern city.

We get out of the cab and Dad strides inside to the reception desk with my little brother, Adom, bouncing beside him, but I'm not ready to go into the lobby yet. I want to find some hint of an older, more magical Egypt. I stand in the circular drive, facing the river. I'm looking at the Nile, I tell myself, and it's not just an exotic name anymore, but a real river, flowing brown and wide before my eyes.

I'm standing there, gawking like the tourist I am, when a small, shriveled woman who looks older than the pyramids sidles up to me. I think she's a beggar, and I'm about to shake my head and tell her I don't have any money when she presses a small, cold object into my hand, holding my fingers tightly closed over it with her own gnarled hand. A gold snake with ruby eyes circles her wrist and I can't stop staring at the elegant bracelet, so out of place on her wrinkled skin. I don't want whatever it is she's forced into my hand—I want the bracelet, with a sudden, piercing hunger. I'm not the kind of girl who cares much about jewelry, so I can't explain the yearning ache that comes out of nowhere.

"Please, tell me where could I buy . . ." I point to the bracelet, but she shakes her head and stares at me with piercing black eyes. Then she nods as if satisfied, loosens her grip, and walks away, leaving a cloud of spicy scent behind and the image of the golden snake seared into my memory. I sniff hungrily, smelling cardamom, pepper, and a trace of some herb. It smells like the Egypt I imagined.

Who was that old woman? What did she want? I open my hand. A stone carving rests in my palm. Although the day is hot, the small sculpture is chilled, as if it's been buried underground for a long time. It's a model of some kind of building, like the miniature Colosseums and Parthenons I've seen sold on tourist stands in Italy and Greece. Except this isn't some cheap, plastic, mass-produced souvenir, and I have no idea what it represents. It's not a place I know, but the carving is clearly a work of art. There are three stories to it, each one slightly smaller than the one below, with beautifully detailed columns. I can even see the suggestions of carvings on the tiny walls. Small statues head the ramps that join the tiers. The stone has a translucent golden glow, capturing the sunlight that touches it. This, I realize, is how I pictured Cairo, something like this. The stone seems to throb in my hand like a living creature. It isn't the bracelet I wanted so desperately, but it has just as much magical presence. I take out my sketchbook, sit on the bench by the hotel entrance, and start to draw the carving.

"Cool!" Adom's voice startles me just as I've finished my drawing, and I quickly close my hand over the carving. "Where did you get that? What is it? Let me see!"

"I don't know what it is," I say, opening my hand again. "But it's amazing. Look at all the detail!"

"Where'd you get it?" Adom asks again.

"An old woman gave it to me." I don't believe it myself, even as I say it. It seems like it magically appeared in my hand, perfect and whole.

"Talibah, Adom—there you are!" Dad walks out into the glare of the day and shields his eyes from the sun. "Come on, our rooms are ready. Let's get settled, then we can explore a little."

I don't know why, but I don't show him the carving. It feels like a secret somehow, and I slip it into my backpack along with the sketchbook. Adom sees me and understands. He doesn't say anything to Dad, either.

That night I have a strange dream. I'm in a dark corridor, the air stale and warm, tasting of dust and clay. "Find him," a woman's voice says. The walls are alive with the grimacing faces of demons, plodding herds of cows, and dancers swaying, but when I try to look closer, the figures melt and blur, shifting into new forms—from fish leaping out of a river to a procession of men with animal heads. Where am I? And where is the voice coming from? "Find him!" it demands, more urgent than before.

"Who?" I yell. "Find who?" There's no answer, only the endless corridor and the constantly changing shapes on the walls. "Who?" I shout again. And then I wake up—the painted corridor is gone, along with the commanding voice.

It takes me a minute to remember I'm not at home, but in the hotel. I rub my eyes, trying to clear out the sleep and the sense that I've forgotten something important, something the dream demanded from me. What is it? What am I supposed to do?

"Find him!" What does it mean? I don't know anyone who's missing. Adom is asleep in the bed next to mine, snoring so loudly I'm surprised I was ever able to fall asleep. And Dad's in his own room next door. There's no other "him," only the strange echo of the dream.

Even though it's still dark, there's no way I can get back to sleep. Instead, I get dressed, thinking everything will seem more normal as soon as dawn comes. I can't shake the feeling that I've forgotten something important, like a final exam or a permission slip. Maybe the feeling has to do with being in Egypt for the first time. Mom and Dad were both born here, but we never visited their old home, maybe because we don't have any relatives left here, except for distant cousins. Dad's parents live in New York, near us. I never knew my other grandparents, since they died when Mom was young. And all our other relatives are spread around the world. Dad has a brother in Morocco, another in India, and a sister in Jordan.

Now that Mom's been dead for five years, now that I'm fourteen and Adom, the baby of the family, is ten, Dad finally realized he wanted to show us his native country. Dad's a historian, specializing in ancient Egyptian literature. His work was the main reason for this trip. Since his meetings coincided with our spring break, he decided to take us with him, something I think he should have done long ago. I've wanted to see Egypt ever since Mom showed me photos of the pyramids when I was little, but it was always "next year" or "when your brother is older." We waited so long for the perfect time that it never came—with Mom, that is. Yes, I'm in Egypt, but I never got to go with her.

For Dad, it's a return to a familiar, beloved home. He's excited to be here and promises us we'll have a wonderful time. After begging to come here for so long, I'm still waiting for that to happen. Except for the old woman and the strange carving, Cairo isn't what I expected. And it's clear it's not my home, like I'd hoped. I may look Egyptian, but I can't speak fluent Arabic. When people talked to me yesterday, most of their words were just piping tones to me—even when I understood small fragments, nothing made sense.

Despite all that's strange, I have to admit there are parts that seem oddly familiar. The landscape here— the tall palm trees, the brown ribbon of the Nile River cutting through the city, the dusty smell of the air—none of it is at all like New York, but somehow I recognize it. Maybe it's because of all the stories about Egypt Grandma's told me. Maybe the words have sunk deep into my bones. Maybe they swim in my veins so that I'm part of this country, too, whether I feel it or not. At least, I want that to be true.

I draw back the edge of the curtain and watch the orange glow of the sun rising between the slender palms on the other side of the Nile. It's almost morning. For a second, the tall tree trunks look like gold-tipped obelisks balancing the golden sun between them. Obelisks in downtown Cairo? When I blink my eyes, the obelisks vanish, and the familiar palm trees are back where they belong. First I dream of voices, now I'm seeing things.

I feel my forehead, but I don't seem feverish. Maybe I just want so much for this place to be magical, like what I expected, like what it promised to be with the old woman, and I'm imagining it that way. I sigh. I wish there *were* obelisks across the river. I wish a genie would fly by on a magic carpet. Instead, I'm trapped in a bland, ordinary hotel room. I could be in Anywhere, USA, not in the capital of Egypt.

The obelisks are gone, but I draw them while I can remember what they looked like. Maybe the only place I'll find the Egypt of my dreams is in my sketchbook.

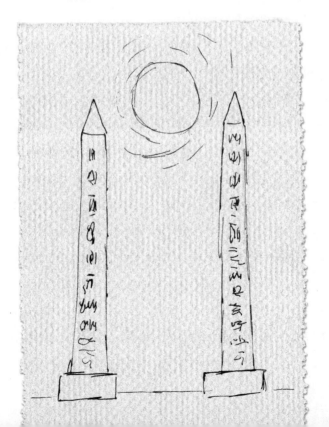

At breakfast in the hotel restaurant, Dad bubbles over with plans. "Today we'll go to the museum—it's one of the greatest in the world. Everyone knows about King Tut's treasure, but there's so much else to see! I want to show you some of the beautiful papyrus manuscripts on display."

Dad's writing a book on the most common ancient Egyptian papyrus, the Book of the Dead, so I'm not surprised that manuscripts are on the top of his Must See list. "And there are some new artifacts exhibited that recently turned up on eBay and were confiscated by the Egyptian government."

"On eBay? Cool!" Adom says. "Now you can get the mummy's curse over the Internet!"

"Don't be ridiculous." Dad laughs. "There is no curse. You've been watching too many bad movies." He tries to look serious, but I can see the edge of a smile on his lips. "And it's no joke to see stolen antiquities for sale, even in cyberspace." Then he turns to me. "And you, Talibah, aren't you excited to see these things?"

I look up from the eggs I've been scraping from one side of my plate to the other. I'm trying not to think about Mom, how she's not here with us, but the eggs don't distract me, and no matter how much

I rearrange them, they don't look appetizing. "Huh? I mean, yeah."

"You must be tired," Dad says. "Jet lag, I'm sure. Did you sleep okay?"

I hate it when he tells me how I'm feeling, as if I don't know myself. I can predict what Dad will say if I start on my brother's snoring, so I just nod my head. *He* can figure out whether I'm nodding yes to being tired or yes to sleeping okay.

Dad dumps a fresh slice of toast on my plate. "Eat something. You're going to need a lot of energy to handle all the big plans we have today."

That's Dad's answer to any problem—eat something. But the toast looks better than the eggs, so I pick it up and nibble on a corner. Anyway, I know how exhausting museums are, especially if my father's leading the tour. He's dragged us to museums all our lives and there's no point whining about yet another stuffy old building crammed with paintings and sculptures. When Dad says you're going to a museum, there's no escape. It's the price Adom and I pay for being able to travel to amazing places.

I finish the toast and some strong, sugary tea. Now I'm awake and ready to go, while Adom is buttering his fifth slice of bread. That boy can really pack it away. If it were up to him, we'd eat breakfast until it was time for lunch, then start all over again. Dad's busy poring over the train schedule and map, figuring out when to leave for Luxor. He doesn't care that Adom's stuffing his face with more food than a camel could stow in its hump.

"Can we go now?" I ask, sick of waiting for Mr. Eat-It-All to finish.

Dad looks up from the notebook, where he's been jotting down notes. It's like he's the one who's been caught in a dream and is suddenly waking up, noticing that we're here, waiting to do something more interesting than eating.

"Ah, the two of you are ready? Yes, let's get going. So much to see, so much to do." He pushes back his chair noisily. "Come, come, the museum is just a short walk away, no need for a cab."

"That's a relief!" I say. "People drive like maniacs here! It's a wonder there aren't more accidents." No one pays attention to the concept of lanes or intersections. It's like the lines on the road are suggestions, not guides to where the cars should go. I wouldn't be surprised to see a car drive on the sidewalk or into the hotel lobby!

"Ah, but there are accidents." Dad winks at me.

"Constantly, so many no one pays them any mind. But we don't have to worry about that. Until we cross the street." He winks again, this time at Adom.

Dad's right. The museum is very close, just around the corner, so we don't have to brave the rushing flood of cars, donkey carts, and people. As soon as we walk into the vast entrance hall, my heart starts pounding furiously, like it does when I glimpse Casey Moreno in the halls at school. It's like a tug deep inside me, a pull drawing me into the museum. There's something for me here—suddenly I'm sure. It's not my imagination, and I doubt it's a boyfriend.

The Sphinx Speaks

U SUALLY A MUSEUM IS AN ESCAPE FROM THE noisy rush of city streets. It's quiet inside the Cairo museum, but just as chaotic as outside—a still version of the same jumbled disorder. I'm used to museums that are chilly, majestic spaces with art evenly distributed on the walls, sculptures lined up with a clean discipline, cases of smaller objects organized so that the smallest fragment of pottery displayed is labeled and explained. The museum in Cairo is more like an old, eccentric aunt's attic or a giant yard sale, except everything is beyond old. Objects from thousands of years ago are plopped down in the rooms in no order that I can figure out, some identified with yellowed bits of paper, others not described at all, so that you're left to guess what it is you're looking at.

It's exactly the kind of museum that Adom loves. I can tell he's imagining that he's rummaging through a pirate's lair where treasures from exotic voyages have been heaped up while waiting for the captain's return with yet more loot. To me, it's more like entering a haunted house. The dusty cobwebs add to the spooky atmosphere, and I can almost hear chains clanking in the ghostly distance. The air is heavy with ancient secrets. I feel sharply alert, as if I expect to bump into a ghost or a mummy risen from the dead.

Dad inhales loudly. "Ah," he pronounces in that professorial tone he has, "smell that? That, my children, is the perfume of Egypt—her stones, her papyri, her golden riches. The history of Egypt is all here, from the earliest times before the pyramids to Cleopatra and the Romans who followed her."

Adom sniffs. "Smells like they haven't vacuumed or dusted in a long time. I love this place! Next time you nag me to clean my room, I'll say I'm doing things the Egyptian way."

Dad smiles. "Nice try. Now let's see some art!" He rubs his palms together. He's as excited as Adom in a candy store. All the dusty sculptures are like brightly colored treats to Dad. Sometimes I wish I could see art the way he does. When I was little, I imagined that if I wore his glasses, I'd have his vision of things. Now I know it doesn't work that way. Still, he does his best to train our eyes, to get us to understand what we're looking at. That's hard to do in such a disorganized mess. I don't know what to look at first, but naturally Dad knows exactly where to go.

"This place is enormous, so we can't see everything. We must pick and choose. And what I choose first is some papyri I've been studying. Come this way." He strides past stone reliefs; enormous, looming statues; and cases full of pottery, jewelry, and cylinder seals. Adom darts from case to case while trying to keep up. I walk more slowly, worried I'll miss something important, though I don't know what it could be. The carved faces we pass remind me of last night's dream—the farther we go, the more I feel like the air is thickening like freezing water, holding me in its stillness.

Dad stops abruptly in a small room lined with cases holding unwound rolls of papyrus. "These," he says, falling into his accustomed museum lecture mode, "are copies of the Book of the Dead. Remember, you've seen ones like these in Paris at the Louvre museum."

We both know this is Dad's favorite topic. "Yes," Adom says, "I remember. This is a nice one here." He points to a scroll. "It spells out how to cross from this world to the next. Here's the soul being weighed."

"And who is that?" Dad indicates a jackal-headed man, standing next to the scale.

"Easy!" pipes Adom. "That's Anubis, the god of the dead. After a person dies, he meets the soul and leads it to be tested. If the heart is heavier than a feather, then it's full of evil and the soul's not allowed to pass on to Paradise—that's the Field of Reeds."

"Very good!" Dad beams with pride. "Talibah, what is that?" He points to a creature that is part hippo, part crocodile, part lion.

I know my part as well as Adom does. "That's a demon. It devours the bad souls." I sketch the scene. It's funny how drawing the scale, the gods, the demons, I feel like I'm there, next to the soul being weighed.

"Cool!" Adom has heard all this many times, but he's still fascinated. He loves all the monsters and demons. There are so many, he can't keep track of them all. "How about that thing? I don't remember seeing it before. What is it?" He points to a different lion-headed beast.

"Before the heart is weighed, the soul has to first pass several tests," Dad explains. He's in full professor voice now. Sometimes I think we should get grades for listening to him, though a snack in the museum café would be a better reward. "If the dead person doesn't know the right names to call the gods that guard the ten gates, demons such as this one eat the soul. The Book of the Dead instructs you so you know all the proper names, allowing you to pass through to the Hall of Justice, where the soul is finally weighed."

"I love that there's a guidebook to the afterlife," Adom says. "The ancient Egyptians really had death figured out."

Dad nods. "At least they believed they had. You know, of course, that the reason for the pyramids, for the mummies, for all the rich objects placed in the pharaohs' tombs was because the ancient Egyptians believed that the soul, the *ka*, lived on after the body's death. It was important to preserve the body and to leave it with what it would need to nourish it in the afterlife. Tombs were filled with clothing, jewelry, furniture, even chariots, as well as sculptures of food and many, many servants—the *ushabti* figures that fill so many museum shelves all over the world. And the guide for all this, the how-to manual for moving from this life to the next, was the Book of the Dead."

"But where did the soul go if it followed all the right directions?" I ask, surprising myself. I can't help thinking of Mom. I was so worried that she'd get lost in the afterlife that I slipped a paperback copy of the Book of the Dead into her coffin. I figured Dad wouldn't notice that it was missing, and anyway, Mom needed it more than he did. After the funeral, I remember asking Dad what had happened to her, was she in heaven? Where did the dead go? And did all of you die along with your body? Dad didn't have textbook answers then. I was left without a mother and without a place I could even imagine her except in the cold, hard ground. Maybe here, now, years later, I would get the answer I was searching for then.

"Sometimes the soul could be reborn into another body, but that was taking the chance of enduring a life of suffering," Dad says. "Sometimes it went to the Field of Reeds, the Egyptian idea of heaven. That was clearly preferred. The idea was that wherever it went, the soul could always return to the tomb, to all the riches there, to feed and care for itself."

"Did Mom read the Book of the Dead before she died so she'd know all the right names? Did she go to the Field of Reeds? What would her spirit do without a tomb full of stuff to use? Where would she go?" Adom's thinking the same things I am, only I don't dare mention Mom. I know Dad doesn't like to talk about her. Usually Adom doesn't either. I guess all this stuff about the dead makes him think of the only dead person he knows, although he was so little when she died, he hardly remembers Mom at all. I was nine then, old enough that I can't forget her.

Even now, five years after her death, Dad rarely mentions Mom. Considering what a big deal the ancient Egyptians are to him, with their insistence on keeping alive people's names and memories after they died, Dad's attitude is especially strange. He's sealed up stories about Mom and buried them deep down inside himself. There's only one photograph of her in the house that's out in the open and it's on top of his bedroom dresser. Adom used to ask Dad all the time what Mom was like, her hair, her face, her voice, what she liked to do, what she'd done with us. Dad's responses got shorter and shorter until they weren't answers at all and Adom stopped asking. Mom is the one subject Dad doesn't like to lecture on, the one question he won't even try to answer.

Today is no different. Dad changes the topic away from Mom and back to ancient history. "We're talking about how the Book of the Dead was used at the time that it was written, not now. If the tomb was broken into and the goods there were stolen, as often happened, the ancient Egyptians believed that the soul would wander, unnourished, looking for a shrine where prayers might be said for it and offerings might be left for it to feed on. Of course, the soul didn't need actual food and drink, just the idea of it. That's why images on walls or clay representations were enough."

Adom gets the hint. He sees how Dad's mouth has tightened, hears how his voice has stiffened. His next questions aren't ones he really cares about—they're an offering to Dad, meant to reassure him that we won't talk about Mom anymore. We're safely on the subject of antiquity again.

"Is that what the mummy's curse is about? Revenge for stealing the soul's stuff? And does that mean the soul is in the mummy itself?" Adom keeps his own voice bright. I'm impressed that at ten, he already knows how to take care of Dad this way.

Dad forces a laugh, and we all try to relax. The dangerous quicksand topic of Mom has been avoided. "I don't know about the mummy's curse. Although the ancients did believe in magic and often cast spells to protect and seal the tombs. Whether they worked or not is another matter." He shrugs. "I suppose if they did, this entire museum would be doomed, filled as it is with objects taken from royal tombs."

I can't help shivering. All this stuff about the soul living on and returning to its tomb gives me the creeps. Does that mean that the voice in my dream belongs to some ancient Egyptian? I shake my head, feeling ridiculous. Why would some old dead Egyptian haunt me? Then I have a really creepy thought—if anyone's haunting me, wouldn't it be Mom? Is it her voice I heard in the dream? I wish I could remember what she sounded like, but I can't. I haven't been able to for years.

I try to focus on what Dad's saying, but the words ring hollow in my ears, sounds without any meaning. I watch him and Adom as the air between us starts to waver and blur. I blink, but a strange fog hovers between us. Suddenly I feel dizzy and need to lean on the case in front of me to keep from falling. I stare at the papyrus displayed inside and try to focus on the painting of animal-headed people lined up on either side of a scale where a heart is being weighed. The colors are vivid and rich, the ink lines crisp and dark. I feel a chill and the fog thickens—softening the world beyond the edges of the scroll until the museum falls away, everything falls away, and I'm in the papyrus itself.

"Come forth and be weighed," a deep voice calls. Anubis, the jackal-headed god of death towers over me. "Come forth!" Anubis repeats, louder this time.

"But I'm not dead!" I protest. "I don't belong here!"

"The time to measure your life has come!" the jackal thunders. His sharp black muzzle gapes open, revealing jagged, glistening teeth.

Something jabs me in the ribs.

"Hey," grunts Adom. "Move over! You're blocking the whole case. What are you trying to do anyway, shove your whole body in there?"

I don't know what to think. The jackal-god is gone. The lines and colors of the papyrus no longer surround me, but lie flat on the scroll, where they belong.

"I'm sorry," I say. "I just, um. I don't know—this papyrus seems so real. It makes me dizzy trying to take it all in." I don't want them to think I'm crazy, though I'm wondering myself.

Dad smiles proudly at me. Thinking a scroll is coming to life isn't going nuts in his view. It's art appreciation. "Yes, well, it is a powerful papyrus. And you have it in your blood to feel the strength of such images."

"What do you mean?" His words make me shudder.

"Well, you are your father's daughter, aren't you? Don't I specialize in exactly this kind of thing?" Dad sweeps his arm out, gesturing to the cases of scrolls all around us.

"I hope that's all it is," I groan. "Either that or I've caught some strange third-world disease."

Dad shakes his finger at me. "This is something you should be proud of, young lady! You have a profound connection to these works of art because this history runs through your veins. You may have been born in the United States, but you're both Egyptian. You can fight it or embrace it, but the link cannot be broken."

I shrug, but I wonder if he's right. Is Mom trying to tell me something through the Book of the Dead?

Is she trying to reach me there, in the place where she belongs? I've often daydreamed about talking to Mom, seeing her again, asking her what she thinks of me now, but I'm not eager to meet a ghost, even hers. Maybe I'm just jet-lagged, like Dad suggested at breakfast. No jackal-headed god talked to me. I wasn't really caught in an ancient painting like Alice sucked into Wonderland through the rabbit hole. I'm tired, that's all. At least that's what I tell myself. Actually, I feel strangely energetic, as if my eyes are wide open.

I follow Dad and Adom out of the papyrus gallery and through several halls until we come to the coolly modern wing that houses the treasures of King Tut. The glassed-in rooms reserved for the famous boy king are sleek and spare, showing off the tomb's riches in elegantly designed cases. It's like we've been transported ahead in time to a different century entirely. I almost expect a robotic voice to guide us through the exhibit, or at least a rack of those tour headphones that sprout all over museums.

"Well, of course, we must see this," Dad says, taking the place of any recorded commentary. "Tutankhamen wasn't a powerful or important pharaoh, so if these things seem luxurious and beautiful, just imagine what kinds of articles would be in the tomb of a mighty pharaoh like Ramses II or Hatshepsut."

"Who?" The name sends an electric charge through me. It seems oddly familiar, though I don't think I've ever heard it before. "Hatshepsut?" The word feels like a whispered secret on my tongue. "Who was he?"

"Ah, you mean who was *she*. Hatshepsut lived during the New Kingdom, in the Eighteenth Dynasty, around 1470 BC. She's best known for being the only woman pharaoh, and a strong one at that. Cleopatra doesn't count—she was a weak figurehead of the Romans, long after the height of Egypt's power. Hatshepsut is famous for expanding trade and peace—and for her mortuary temple, which is an architectural masterpiece like nothing that came before or since. It has three terraces, connected by ramps, like a broad, flattened step pyramid. I'll tell you more about her when we go to her temple. Now we should be thinking about Tut."

I can't focus on anything except Hatshepsut. Dad's description of her temple reminds me of something, but I can't think of what. Where have I seen three terraces before? I try to recapture last night's vivid dream, but the setting for that was dark corridors, like in a tomb, not open terraces in a temple. Dad is so intent on explaining the photos of the excavation of King Tut's tomb to Adom, he doesn't even notice when I slip out of the modern gallery and back into the dark disarray of the main museum. I don't know what I'm looking for, except it has something to do with Hatshepsut—though, big as the museum is, it couldn't house her whole temple. Maybe I'm looking for her mummy. Whatever it is, my feet seem sure of where to go and I let them take me past several millennia of sculpture and mummies. As I turn a corner, a slender gold circlet in a glass case catches my eye. Coming closer I recognize the ruby-eyed snake bracelet worn by the old woman. I'm lucky this is one of the cases that has an identifying label—a yellowed card describes in English and Arabic that the jewelry dates from the Eighteenth Dynasty, during the reign of Hatshepsut. The text is old and faded, but I can still read it:

This asp bracelet was worn by the Servants of Hatshepsut, a token of their devotion to the Pharaoh which would outlast death. The dedicated few who survived the initiation rites to this special group swore to serve Hatshepsut for all eternity, passing on the secrets of the Pharaoh from father to son, from mother to daughter, in a never-ending circle of devotion, aptly symbolized by the golden serpent.

So that's where the woman found such an elegant bracelet—in the museum gift shop! Seeing it again makes me want it even more. I hope it doesn't cost too much. Or if it does, that I can convince my father to buy it for me. I read the label over and over again, as if memorizing it will make the bracelet mine. It isn't until I've whispered the words to myself for the fourth time that I realize I'm reading about Hatshepsut, and once again I feel a jolt of recognition. Hatshepsut—I still need to find something of hers.

I pull myself away from the case, and start walking down the gallery. Was that what my feet were so drawn to, the bracelet? Was that what I was looking for? My pace quickens and I'm sure there's something else I need to find. And there it is, right in front of me—a sphinx, a human-headed lion, like the Great Sphinx that's an Egyptian cliché, only much smaller. There are several identical sphinxes lined up in a row. I lean over to read the faded typewritten label: Sphinx from the entry walkway to Deir El-Bahri, the

Mortuary Temple of Hatshepsut. There's that name again—Hatshepsut! I wanted to see her temple, and here I've found sculptures that came from it. I stare at the sphinx's face, then start to draw it. Sometimes when I'm sketching, following the contours with my eyes and pen, I feel connected to the thing I'm drawing. I want to get a better sense of Hatshepsut, but even though the sphinx's face is supposedly a portrait of the pharaoh herself, it's so stylized that I can't see anything of the person who was Egypt's only woman pharaoh.

Who was she, I wonder, searching the stone features for an answer. Slowly the granite eyelids blink. Did I imagine that? As if to answer me, they blink again and the stone lips move, speaking in the voice from my dream. "Find him! Find him!" the sphinx hisses. The muscles under the lion's taut skin ripple, the claws on the massive paws flex out. I want to run but my feet are frozen. I can't move. I stare, horrified, as the lion rocks back on its hindquarters and starts to stand up, like a giant cat stretching after an eons-long nap. It feels as if I'm pulling my legs out of drying cement, but I manage to turn and run, faster than I've ever run before. I'm afraid to look back, expecting to feel the hot breath of the lion-creature on my neck at any moment.

I dart between cases and around corners until I run smack into a man. I look behind me, but there's no sign of the sphinx. I listen for footsteps in the silence. Nothing.

The man says something to me in Arabic.

"I'm sorry," I say, looking at him for the first time. "I don't understand." He's probably around forty, with thick eyebrows and crow-black hair. He's dressed in what I call professor clothes—a tweed coat and brown pants with a thin, bland tie of no particular color or pattern. In other words, he's dressed like my dad, except Dad skips the tie when we travel.

The man straightens his glasses and dusts off his sleeves as if I'd brought the desert sands into the gallery with me. "No harm done," he says mildly in perfect English, "though I wonder why you would run in a museum. This is not a gymnasium, you know."

"Yes, I know. It's just . . . just . . ." What can I say? That I imagined a sphinx was about to leap off of its plinth and devour me? "It's just," I try again and the words tumble out without my thinking. "It's just that I lost my father and brother in the King Tut galleries and I was in a hurry to get to them again."

The man leans toward me in a courtly bow. "Allow me then to help you find them. My name is Rashid Khalfani. And you are?"

He's polite in an old-fashioned way, but something about the man's eyes, the tightness to his mouth reminds me of a giant cobra. I want to ignore him, to just walk away, but instead I tell him my name, Talibah Mahmoud. As soon as I say it, I wonder if I'm giving too much information to a total stranger, especially one who has a serpentine something about him. I should have invented a name like I do when I don't want a stranger to know who I am. I have a whole list of fake names and phone numbers that I've memorized, so I won't even hesitate when I lie. That's the trick to sounding like you're telling the truth. But it's too late now.

"Mahmoud? Anwar Mahmoud's daughter?" The

man laughs. "Why, this is an extraordinary coincidence! I knew that your father was here—he wrote to tell me, and we made plans to see each other, though not for today. This is an unexpected treat, to meet his darling daughter so soon after your arrival." The man stares at me as if he's trying to read something in my face. I hope he doesn't see my embarrassment that I almost lied to him. I wonder what my dad would have said if I'd introduced myself as Brandi LaRue, one of my favorite aliases. "You look more like your mother than your father—you have her almond eyes and broad cheeks—but still I should have recognized you. That tangle of curly hair is just like your grandmother's! Our families have been close for generations. My father was your grandfather's best friend, and your father and I knew each other growing up in Cairo. We both became Egyptologists, too, though I excavate tombs while your father, of course, studies manuscripts."

Normally I would be curious about someone who knew my parents when they were younger. The name Khalfani is vaguely familiar. I can't remember who mentioned the family to me—Grandma, Grandpa, Mom, or Dad—but I've heard stories about so many close friends and relatives, they all blend together. I've only met a family friend once, a distant cousin who had business in New York and spent the weekend with us, and I can't even be sure what his name was. Was it Khalfani, too? Whoever he was, I was too young to take advantage of meeting him. If it had happened just a couple of years ago, I'd have pumped him for information about what Mom and Dad were like, especially Mom. The last time I saw Dad's brothers and sister was at Mom's funeral. A lot of friends and family came to that, but to be honest, I don't remember anything about it except crying. The Queen of England could have been there, and I wouldn't have noticed.

I should feel lucky to have run into Rashid. I can ask him all the questions about my family I've held inside of me for so long. What was my mom like? What was the most important thing to her, besides her family? What kind of people were her parents? I know they died before my mom left Egypt, but I don't know where they lived or what they did or what their personalities were like. Dad doesn't tell us anything. But I can't stop thinking about the sphinx. Did it really talk? If it did, does that mean the voice from the dream is the sphinx's, not Mom's? Or am I just sleep-deprived?

It's a good thing I don't have to say anything.

Mr. Khalfani seems happy to have a one-sided conversation as he guides me back to the Tut galleries to find Dad and Adom. He chatters about old family friends, vacations taken together, and school-yard pranks. I barely need to nod to keep him going. That's something I've noticed about a lot of grown-ups—they say they want to talk to you, but being with a teenager makes them so uncomfortable they just talk around you instead of having a conversation.

"Rashid! What an unexpected pleasure!" Dad says when he sees me with his old friend. He rushes forward to hug him. "I thought we were meeting for dinner tomorrow, not a museum visit together today! I see you've already met Talibah, and this is my son, Adom."

Adom stretches out his hand politely. Dad has coached him well. "Good to meet you, young man." Rashid beams. "I am Rashid Khalfani, an old friend of the family. Really you should consider me a part of your family, like an uncle, since your father and I were practically raised like brothers."

Dad nods in agreement and slaps Rashid on the back. "Adom, this is precisely the man I was telling you about, the one who is leading an excavation in the Valley of the Nobles."

Adom's eyes sparkle. "A real excavation? You mean a tomb? What have you found? Stuff like this?" He points to the cases of Tut's treasure.

"Perhaps you would like to see for yourself? You are welcome to come to the site. It is the tomb of a powerful noble from the Eighteenth Dynasty, the vizier under Hatshepsut. You know what a vizier is?" Rashid leans toward Adom. "Like a prime minister, the second in command under the king."

There's that name again—Hatshepsut! There are too many odd coincidences piling up—first the old woman and her bracelet, then the dream, the pull of the Book of the Dead, next finding the same bracelet worn by Hatshepsut's servants and the sphinx from her mortuary temple, and now running into the man who happens to be excavating the tomb of the highest government official under the woman pharaoh. But why? What does it all mean? I'm beginning to feel overwhelmed. Why do I have to find "him" anyway? I'm not the one who lost him, whoever he is. I'm not an expert on ancient Egypt. I'm just a kid on vacation! My goal for this trip is to lie by the pool and get a great tan, not run errands for some Egyptian ghost, even if that ghost could be my mother.

A Journey

That night, Rashid joins us for dinner, and he and Dad trade stories about friends and family Adom and I have never met. My brother's eyes glaze over with boredom and I stick headphones in my ears. I don't even pretend to pay attention. By the time dessert is served, Adom has built an elaborate structure from the packets of sugar on the table. When it collapses, Dad looks at my brother as if he's just noticed his existence.

"Adom! That is not proper dinner-table behavior." Dad frowns.

"But I'm not eating. And you aren't talking to us, so why do we have to be here? Can't we go back to our room now?" Adom's voice has a familiar are-we-there-yet whine to it, piercing through the music I'm trying to listen to.

Dad presses his lips together. "Rashid is practically family, and I would think you would want to hear about our relatives here in Egypt."

Adom's eyes flare. "You mean someone's third cousin twice removed? I don't know any of these people! I would rather read a book! Anything but sit here and be bored."

Rashid smiles and squeezes Dad's arm. The gesture strikes me as intimate. Something about it makes me pay attention to Rashid's hand, and that's when I notice the ring he wears. It's heavy and gold with a disc set on top inscribed with some kind of hieroglyphic. It looks like the kind of thing you'd see in a museum case, something not worn by a living person, like the serpent bracelet the old woman wore. When I saw the golden snake, I desperately wanted it, but now, looking at the ring, I'm filled with revulsion. I can't say why—the ring isn't ugly. In fact, it's beautiful. I wonder if Rashid found it when he dug up a tomb. Maybe it carries a mummy's curse or simply the stench of death and that's why it gives me the creeps. The thought of it touching my finger makes my flesh crawl, but Rashid doesn't seem to mind it. Somehow that makes him creepy, too. I want to ask him about it, but I don't dare. Instead, I turn down the volume so I can hear what Rashid says. Under the table, I pull out my sketchbook and draw what the ring looks like.

"He is being a boy, plain and simple. Of course these long lists of names he has never heard before are not interesting to him. But I think I know something that will be." Rashid leans toward Adom, who looks stunned that a stranger would rise to his defense.

"How would you like to see a tomb, a tomb that is still being explored so it is not yet open to the public? It would be like a private VIP tour."

Adom's face splits into an enormous grin, his round

black eyes huge in wonder. "Really? You'll take us? A real tomb with a mummy's curse and everything?"

I shudder in my seat. I've had enough talk about black magic. There's definitely something powerful about Rashid's ring, and not in a good way.

"I do not know about a curse, but there is a mummy, and many other things besides." Rashid turns back to Dad. "I do not know when you plan to arrive in Luxor, but I am taking the train down tomorrow, so any time after that is fine with me."

Dad is smiling now. "You are very kind to include the children. It would be a pleasure and an honor. So tell us about this tomb. I have a feeling this is the kind of story Adom wants to listen to, not details of Auntie Farah's gout or Cousin Jabari's high school graduation."

Adom nods and jabs me in the ribs for the second time today. "Take off those headphones and listen. We get to go to a tomb—while it's still being excavated! It's going to be so cool!"

"Ow!" I grumble, tucking away the headphones. "So what's this tomb Adom's talking about?" I ask.

"Remember I told you that I am excavating the tomb of Hapuseneb, the vizier under Hatshepsut?" Rashid says, fixing his eyes on me. His look is disturbing somehow, like he is seeing more of me than I want to show him. "We have uncovered most of the chambers and are recording the contents of the tomb, so you have arrived at a most opportune time. Much of the rubble has been cleared away, but none of the objects has yet been removed."

None? What about the ring, I wonder.

"How did you find it?" Dad asks. "I thought the Valley of the Nobles had been thoroughly explored."

"Yes and no." Rashid's thick eyebrows lift like wings on his broad forehead. "The valley is so rich in tombs that many remain to be discovered. Still, it is not easy to find those that are yet hidden. I was somehow drawn to this spot. I cannot explain it except to say I felt it in my bones when I walked near the home of the vizier's *ka*, or spirit. I felt pulled to my knees at the place that was almost the precise entrance to the tomb. It was," he pauses dramatically, "a compelling experience."

I'm annoyed that Rashid's still looking at me. I can't tell if it's just the usual ickiness I feel when men stare at my chest, or something else. Whatever it is, I can't wait to get away from him.

I open my mouth in an exaggerated yawn. "Excuse me," I say. "I'm so tired, I just can't keep my eyes open anymore. May we be excused?" Dad's much more likely to say yes if I follow his etiquette rules.

"Of course, of course," Dad quickly agrees. "Take your brother and make sure he washes up—with soap—and brushes his teeth."

"With toothpaste," I add. Dad says the same thing every time he puts me in charge of Adom at night. You'd think he'd trust by now that I've got the bedtime ritual down pat. We say a quick good night to Dad and Rashid, and head for the elevators. I'm not a big person—one of the few things Dad says about Mom is that I inherited her slender build—and I feel even smaller in the elaborate gilt car. Suddenly, I'm completely exhausted. Adom, however, is energized at the thought of the tomb, and he jabbers all the way back to our room, chattering even as he brushes his teeth and splashes some water on his face. I let his words lap over me like waves on the beach. I'm not really listening, just letting the sounds soothe me. I'm thinking about Hatshepsut. I wonder if all Egyptians feel pulled to different parts of the country's ancient past, the way Rashid felt directed to Hapuseneb's tomb, the way Dad is drawn to certain papyrus scrolls. The way I feel about Hatshepsut. Maybe there's so much old magic in the sands here that wherever you go, you disturb a mystery waiting for the right person to solve it. Maybe I'll find the magical Egypt I expected after all. I just hope it's the good kind of magic.

I tuck Adom into the bed next to mine, his face smelling like toothpaste and soap. That doesn't mean he really scrubbed or brushed. He knows that if he doesn't smell clean, I make him wash up all over again until he does. He calls it the toothpaste test. I lean down to kiss him, but he tells me to wait, he's not done talking.

"Yes, you are," I tell him. "I know you're excited about the tomb, and it's all very cool, but right now you need to sleep or you won't have the energy to see anything tomorrow."

"We're not going to the tomb tomorrow," Adom protests, "and I always have energy."

"Well, I don't. You need to sleep so I can. Okay?" I kiss his forehead. "You can tell me more in the morning."

"Okay," he grumbles, closing his eyes and pulling the cover up to his ear the way he likes it. I turn out the light, but now that I'm alone with my thoughts, I'm not at all tired. When I close my eyes, images of the Book of the Dead, the sphinx, and Rashid's ring fill the darkness. There's no way to sleep with those pictures in my head.

I try my old trick for calming myself—staring at the ceiling and counting backward from one hundred—but as I drone eighty-seven, eighty-six, eighty-five, the ceiling seems to lower itself, looming closer and closer. Panic surges through me—the room is a tomb closing in on me! I jump out of bed and immediately the ceiling is back where it belongs.

"If this is jet lag, I'm not sure I ever want to travel again," I mutter, willing my heart to stop pounding wildly. I check on Adom, who as usual fell asleep as soon as his eyes closed. I wish I could do that. Now I'm more wide-awake than ever. I take deep, slow breaths, but I can't shake the feeling of dread, so I go into the bathroom and turn on the light. The gleam of stainless steel faucets and tile is reassuring in its ordinariness. I don't want to leave the comforting bright light, so I decide to take a bath. The hot water is soothing, washing away the dust of the strange visions I've been having. By the time I towel myself dry, I'm too tired to worry about the dreams waiting for me in the deep of the night, and I fall asleep quickly for once, just like my brother.

The dry tickle of Adom's fingers tapping on my shoulder and neck wakes me up. I glare at him out of one sleepy eye, the other pressed closed against the pillow.

"Do you always have to poke, prod, jab, squeeze, or pinch me?" I groan. The room is gray with early morning light and I'm relieved that I can't remember any dreams.

Adom shrugs. "Sorry. Dad wanted me to wake you up. Would you rather I yelled in your ear or poured a glass of cold water over your head?"

I glance at the alarm clock. "Six o'clock! Why do we have to be up so early? No museum is open at this hour."

There's a quick knock at the door and Dad walks in, his hair still damp from the shower.

"Good, I see you're both awake. There's been a change in plans. Rashid and I talked it over last night and since he's leaving for Luxor this morning, it makes sense for the two of you to go with him. I have three days of meetings, which would be boring for you, so he has generously offered not only to take you to Hapuseneb's tomb, but to show you around. He'll take you to the great temples at Luxor and Karnak and the funerary sites on the west bank of the Nile—you know, the Valley of the Kings, the Valley of the Queens. You'll get to see all the tombs that the public can go in, as well as those in his private VIP tour. I've made reservations for you at the Garden Palace Hotel. Rashid will be staying at a place close by so he can check on you easily."

"We don't need anyone to check on us," I object. "You've left me in charge of Adom when you've gone on business trips. Remember when you were in San Francisco for three days? We did fine."

"I'm not doubting your abilities, Talibah," Dad insists. "But Egypt is different from being at home in New York. I'd like Rashid to be in charge this time."

When Dad uses that tone, there's no point in arguing, but I'm hurt that he doesn't trust me, that he's treating me like a little kid. I want to take care of us, and until we get to the train station I'm sure I can do it. Then I see what Dad means by Egypt being different from New York. The station is a chaotic throng of peddlers, beggars, and travelers. There are so many people—some milling aimlessly about, some dragging luggage, some herded together in large tour groups, others hawking snacks, drinks, and newspapers—that I'm relieved Dad is there to shove our way through the crowd and lead us to our reserved compartment. Rashid is already there, waiting for us, and he heaves our bags onto the rack over our heads. I'm glad he's with us—he can figure out where to get off the train and how to get to the hotel. I can relax and enjoy the trip.

I love traveling by train and so does Adom. He

bounces up and down on the seat, excited by the journey almost as much as by the tomb we're going to see. I sit next to him, by the window, my headphones already in my ears to block out the rest of the world.

Dad settles some last-minute details with Rashid, and then he leans over and pulls off my headphones.

"I want to make sure you're paying attention. Remember to call me when you get to the hotel and look for something wonderful to tell me about." He pulls Adom to him in a bear hug. "Listen to your sister and to Rashid."

Adom lets Dad hold and kiss him. "Of course, Dad, don't worry."

"And you, take good care of your brother." Dad gathers me in a tight hug. "And of yourself."

"I always do." I try to reassure him. "Come on, Dad, it's only three days. We'll see you soon."

"Yes, I know. And we'll talk before then." He hugs Rashid, too. "*Inshallah*, God willing."

The whistle blows and Dad hurries off the train, waving wildly to us from the platform. Adom leans out the window and waves back until Dad melts into the crowd at the station, then disappears entirely as the train picks up speed and chugs forward, south along the

Nile into the heart of Egypt, the real Egypt of tombs and mummies and mysteries. I draw our route in my sketchbook, copying places listed in the guidebook. We're passing by the Giza pyramids, but ahead of us lie ancient temples, including, I'm sure, Hatshepsut's.

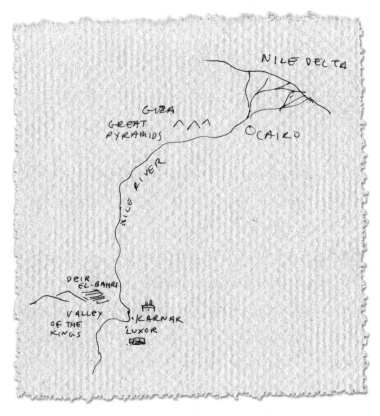

4

Sandscapes

I PRESS MY FACE AGAINST THE WINDOW, TRYING to get as far from Rashid as possible. I remind myself that having him around makes travel easier, but it doesn't feel that way now. For the past two hours he's insisted on bringing us tea, candy, and magazines. Along with each item, he presents me with a thin smile that someone must have once told him was attractive, because it certainly isn't natural. Adom is happy to drink the tea and gobble down the rolls, but I don't want to accept anything, no matter how much my stomach grumbles. Coming from Rashid, the food seems tainted. Why do I distrust him so much? He hasn't said or done anything wrong except wear a creepy, possibly stolen ring. But there's something about him that smells wrong to me, like cheese that's been in the sun too long.

When he leaves for the dining car on another mission to find something to tempt me, I make a deal with Adom. "If you get Rashid to pay attention to you so he doesn't bother me, I'll let you have first pick of the beds in the hotel room."

Adom doesn't exactly leap at the offer. It's not that he doesn't want to deal with Rashid—he's happy to play cards and pester him with questions about mummies—he's just suspicious of my motives. "Why would you do that? He's not bugging you. He's being nice."

"I know, I know." I try to hide the irritation in my voice. "But he's driving me crazy. I wish he'd just leave me alone."

"You sure you're not trying to get rid of me? I only wanted to play a game of Crazy Eights. Or Gin Rummy, if you like that better."

"No, silly, I don't mind playing cards with you. But I'm tired. I want to sleep."

"So sleep. If you're asleep, Rashid's not going to wake you up. He likes you, I can tell." Adom starts dealing cards for Gin.

"Ugh." I stick out my tongue. "You better not

mean 'like' likes me. That's gross! He's about a million years old."

"He's not as old as a mummy!" Adom says. "But you're right—he's way too old to be your boyfriend. I think he just wants to be family, like an uncle, since he knows Dad so well and he knew Mom, too."

Rashid wants to be part of our family? Sometimes Adom surprises me by the things he notices. That could explain why he acts like he knows us better than he does, like we're best buddies when we've really just met. But I can't shake that first impression I got in the museum—there's something snakelike about Rashid, even if I can't say exactly what.

"Look what I have!" Rashid triumphantly flourishes two ice-cream bars with one hand, while he opens and closes the compartment door with the other. "Delicious cold ice cream! Now who wants chocolate and who wants strawberry?"

"I'm not hungry, but thank you anyway," I say politely, nudging Adom to remind him of his promise.

"I'll take chocolate! Thanks, Rashid!" The more sullen I am, the more enthusiastic Adom is. "Want to play Gin? I just dealt the cards."

"Yes, yes, of course." Rashid hands an ice-cream bar

to Adom, unwrapping the other one for himself. "No sense in wasting perfectly good ice cream." Which is what he said about the tea, the rolls, the cookies, and all the other treats I rejected. I can feel him looking at me, but I ignore him; I'm hunched against the window, my eyes pointedly closed, my headphones sealing me off.

Adom leans forward and whispers so loudly I can hear him, "Don't worry about her. She's a teenager. Dad says they're all like that."

"Oh." Rashid nods. "Like what?"

"You know, moody. Especially before noon. You don't dare talk to Talibah before then if you don't want to get your head bitten off. The later in the day it gets, the nicer she is. She's best late at night, kind of like a hamster." Adom sighs. "Which does me no good because by the time she's really nice, I'm asleep."

I try not to smile. That's exactly how it must seem to Adom, like I'm some kind of vampire whose most interesting transformation happens while he's asleep. I feel a pang about leaving him to Rashid, but I know that as long as Adom has someone to play cards with, it doesn't really matter who the other player is. As for Rashid, he can think I'm rude, so long as he stays far away from me. At first, I'm only pretending to nap, but the motion of the train and the rhythmic slap of cards lull me into really falling asleep.

Almost at once the dream starts again, more vivid and insistent than ever. I'm in a painted hall, like a tomb, and the voice hisses in my ear, "Find him! You're closer, closer. Find him now!" Then I'm outside, sand dunes all around me in a bright blaze of sunshine. I'm approaching a great stone wall. No birds or insects stir. Everything is blanketed in a thick silence. I walk through the entrance and see a pathway lined with sphinxes, like the one in the museum. I hesitate, and the voice speaks again: "Come forward. Come find him. Come!" A broad ramp stretches ahead of me. I hurry past the sphinxes and start up the ramp. I realize it's like one of the ramps joining the three tiers in the little carving the old woman gave me. I'm walking up that stone building. Either it's grown or I've shrunk. When I reach the top, I'm in a completely different place in that illogical way dreams have. Now I'm in an open square framed by lotus-topped columns. At one end, twin obelisks pierce the sky, sheathed in gleaming gold that shines so brightly, it hurts my eyes to look at them. "Find him! Now!" The voice is harsher, more urgent than ever. Where am I supposed to go? I hesitate again, then walk toward the obelisks. A dark figure darts between them. I lick my dry lips, my heart thumping heavily in my chest. I can't make out if it's a man or a woman. I have to get closer. I have to find out. I want to see who the person is and yet I'm terrified to look.

But once I reach the obelisks, no one is there. I circle the two tall spires, listening for footsteps. Nothing. Suddenly there it is again, a tall, cloaked figure in the center of the square I just walked through.

I run back the way I came, even though as I get closer my feet feel heavier and a thick dread falls over me. I don't dare to go any farther. My heart is pounding. I want to wake up but I can't.

"Who are you?" I yell.

The figure throws back its cloak and stands massive and dark before me. It's Anubis, the god in the Book of the Dead, the one who almost ate me in the papyrus gallery.

"Come and be judged," the jackal-headed god intones. "The time to measure your life has come."

Not again! I flail my arms out and hit something cold and hard. My eyes fly open and I'm pulled away from the dream, back into the everyday world, where my hands pound against the cool glass window of the train.

"That was quite a dream you were having," Rashid says gently. "Here, have some water."

I'm so groggy from my dream, so parched from fear, that this time I accept. I take the bottle and drink greedily, keenly aware of the muscles in my throat swallowing, of the water settling coolly in my stomach, of being alive.

Adom stares at me as if I've sprouted horns or an extra eye. "Are you okay? You were saying some really weird stuff."

"I was? What did I say?"

"You were asking somebody what their name was and then you started yelling, 'No, no.' It was pretty creepy." Adom narrows his eyes. "You aren't on drugs, are you?" He's clearly seen too many public service announcements warning parents how to look for drug use in their kids.

I shake my head. "I just had a bad dream. A really strange dream."

Rashid smiles, like nightmares are a good thing. "It is only natural that you would have powerful dreams here. This is a powerful place, and part of you deep inside is connecting with its ancestry."

I roll my eyes. "Yeah, right."

"Sounds more like a case of connecting with diarrhea," Adom teases. "That's deep inside, until it comes out!"

"Ha, ha, very funny," I say. Rashid doesn't know what to make of Adom's joke. Maybe he doesn't understand the word "diarrhea"—or a kid's sense of humor.

The dream leaves my head feeling like it's full of heavy, wet sand. I look out the window, trying to erase the scary images with ordinary, safe reality. Only I can't; the landscape outside is exactly the same as in the nightmare—the same low dunes, the same stands of date palms. I sketch quickly, feeling like I'm capturing my dream on the page. Adom is right. This is getting creepy.

Rashid follows my gaze. "We are getting close now, almost at Luxor, which used to be the ancient city of Thebes. We follow the Nile's path the whole trip. And the way the people live now is not so different from in the time of the pharaohs." Mud huts thatched with palm fronds are scattered along the riverbank. Children, goats, and camels all huddle under the same roof, grabbing shade where they can. "Before I forget," Rashid continues, "I brought this book for you. You may want to read it tonight at the hotel. I hope it interests you." He hands me a small book bound in dark green cloth.

Once again, I take something he offers me, though I plan on giving it right back. I open it up to the title page: "Hatshepsut, the Great Woman Pharaoh, Daughter of Justice." The book seems to vibrate in my hand. I don't want to accept a gift from Rashid, but this is something I can't refuse.

So I tell him thank you. "I'm very interested. This is a history of her life?"

"Exactly." Rashid looks pleased with himself. He's happy he got me something I not only accept, but am actually willing to talk about. I don't want to give him that satisfaction, but my curiosity about Hatshepsut is stronger than my growing revulsion toward Rashid, even though I dread the lecture I know is coming. I don't know why the more time I spend with him, the more I dislike Rashid. It's just a gut feeling I can't shake.

Rashid clears his throat, slicks back his hair, and

starts in. "She is called Daughter of Justice because her pharaoh name, the name she ruled under, was Maatkare, meaning Keeper of *Maat*. *Maat* is the principle of order, which the author of the book loosely translates to Justice. But *Maat* is even more important than that. It is the underlying principle that contains all the order of the world. Without it there is chaos and meaninglessness. It was a fitting name for Hatshepsut."

"Why?" I can't help asking. "Isn't that what all pharaohs do, provide order, the rule of law?"

Rashid shakes his head. "It is not what they focused on most. Every pharaoh picked a name to rule under, actually several names, but there was always one principal name of a strength or trait that the pharaoh wanted to embody. Some linked themselves to Ra, the sun god, like Ramses, others to Osiris or Horus. But Hatshepsut chose *Maat*. Her most important achievement was solidifying the order that her father had restored to the kingdom after the invasions of the Hyksos. And beyond that she expanded Egypt, reaching out to neighboring lands for trade."

I nod. But I wonder if the name means more than that—if she's justifying herself being pharaoh, saying that even though she's a woman, her rule is part of the right order of the universe. And maybe that is what she meant—she's not around to ask. Egyptologists like Rashid are only guessing. I know I'm not an expert, but I'm learning, and I trust my instincts. I could be right. My fingers itch to open the book, to find out more for myself.

"We're here! We're here!" Adom jumps to the window, pointing. "See, we're slowing down. I can see the station."

"Yes, let us gather our things," Rashid says, pulling our bags down from the overhead shelf. "A truly magnificent adventure awaits you. Now you are really in the land of the pharaohs."

My stomach churns sourly. Adom is right—we're here, only now I'm not sure this is where I want to be. It's too close to my dream world to be comfortable.

5

The Keeper of Order

AFTER I TAKE A QUICK SHOWER IN OUR room in the Luxor Garden Palace Hotel—which isn't a palace and doesn't have a garden, just some bushes and benches around a fountain—Adom and I meet Rashid in the lobby. He says it's not too late in the afternoon to go to Karnak, the big temple complex just north of Luxor. We walk out of the dim hotel into the bright day, and Rashid immediately plunges into tour guide mode. It's like having Dad with us, the same kind of historical explanation for every step we take. I wish that I could discover a place on my own for once. What would it be like to explore a monument without hearing a lecture about it? Instead of having someone else interpret how I'm supposed to see the place, I could simply take it in, experience it on my own terms.

I try not to listen to Rashid. It works with Adom. I'm used to blocking out his long, detailed descriptions of how he decided between the grilled cheese sandwich and the chicken teriyaki at the school cafeteria or how his teacher assigned new seats to everyone, putting him two desks behind his best friend and right next to the one kid in class who bugs him the most. I even say "that's cool" or "too bad" at the right moments, so Adom never knows I'm not really paying attention. It's harder to do that with Rashid. His voice doesn't have the same piping, musical quality that makes it so easy to turn Adom's chatter into background music, kind of like a chirping bird. Rashid has the ponderous voice of someone used to having large groups of students hang on every word, the voice of someone who likes to hear himself talk and is sure that you'll enjoy it, too.

So despite myself I hear him explain that the temples of Karnak and Luxor were originally linked by a broad avenue lined with ram-headed sphinxes, the same path we're taking now. Instead of a solemn procession of sphinxes, there's a tangle of modern streets and shops displaying alabaster bowls, gaudily painted miniature mummies, and brightly colored clothes. Here at last are the colors I was searching for in Cairo, but they're not part of the city—they're in tacky souvenir stands. Adom flits ahead, racing from shop to shop and then back to report on his finds, from intricately carved daggers to pickled scorpions in bottles. As we near the temple complex, he stops before a man sitting on the dirt in front of one of the surviving ram-headed lions.

"Adom, come on. I want to go in," I tell him.

"Look!" Adom's voice is high-pitched with excitement.

I wonder what fascinates him about this beggar— we've probably seen thousands of them since the plane landed in Cairo. I'm ready to yank him by the arm, but when I catch up to him, I stop as abruptly as he did.

On the ground in front of the man, a cobra lies coiled. I stare, frozen in horror, as the snake rears up, pushing out its signature hood on either side of its evil-looking head. It sways from side to side just like in the cartoons of snake charmers and goofy-looking snakes. Except this snake is deadly serious.

I take a step back. "Adom," I say in a voice as low and calm as I can make it. "Back away slowly. Very slowly."

The man looks up and grins, showing a wide gap where his front teeth once were. He reaches out and grabs the cobra firmly just below the head and offers it to Adom.

"Want hold my cobra?" he asks in stiff English. "Cobra good, very good. Boy hold?"

"No!" I'm appalled. "Boy *not* hold."

"Why not?" Adom begs. "If he can hold the snake, why can't I?"

"Maybe he's built up immunity to the venom. I bet that's how he lost his teeth. The snake bit him and they fell out from the poison." I speak quickly, hoping the man won't understand such rapid English.

Rashid smiles and shakes his head. "The cobra is harmless. These men know how to extract the venom from the hollow fangs. But if you hold it, then you must pay him. This is how he makes his living—catching cobras, removing the poison, and then impressing tourists with his snakes."

Before I can stop him, the man wraps the cobra around Adom's arm. I believe Rashid's explanation. I know the snake isn't deadly, but still the sight of its coils, almost as thick as the slender arm they wind around, makes me queasy.

"Please, Adom, that's enough. Please, can we go now?"

The man doesn't need to understand English to hear

the panic in my voice. He takes the snake back, smiling. "See, boy good. Snake good."

"Thanks," Adom says, putting a coin in the basket beside the man. He grins at me. "I'm fine."

"Well, I'm not fine," I snap. "I want to see the temple. Isn't that why we came?"

"And that is what we shall do," soothes Rashid. I glare at him—he doesn't have to treat me like a baby. No normal person would want to see a cobra's fangs so close to their little brother, no matter how safe the snake is supposed to be. But Rashid has already forgotten about the cobra. He's back in lecture mode, telling us how many thousands of years it took to build the temple complex, how it was the holiest site in ancient Egypt, and how each pharaoh felt compelled to put his mark on it by adding shrines or halls or temples.

He drones on as we walk through the impressive entrance, but I'm not listening anymore. My attention is caught by twin obelisks rising from the center of the temple site. They're the ones I imagined from the hotel window in Cairo and the ones I saw in the dream on the train! The tips aren't golden, but otherwise the scene is identical, the orange disc of the sun reflecting off the pinkish granite of the spires as it hovers between the tips.

And somehow I know that long ago the obelisks were sheathed in gold, just as I imagined them. As I sketch them, I feel like I'm remembering a place I've been to before.

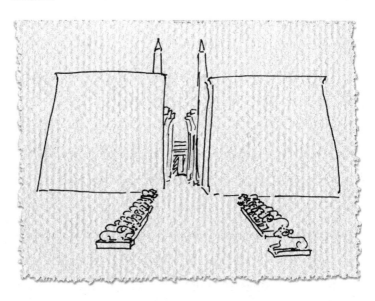

"Magnificent, are they not?" Rashid's voice startles me. I'd forgotten about him and Adom. "The pink granite is an especially beautiful stone and comes from a quarry near Aswan. That means they had first to be cut and then ferried on barges many miles down the Nile until they were brought here. It took three rows of boats, ten boats in a row to pull each obelisk. A thousand men were needed for the job. Then came the difficult task of pulling them upright until they came to rest as you see them now." Rashid pauses and gives me that look again, the one that seems to see right through me. "They were erected by Hatshepsut to celebrate her Jubilee, a triumphal year in her reign, and at the time they were the tallest obelisks in Egypt, impressively covered in gold leaf. The man in charge of this enormous effort was someone especially dear to the pharaoh." Rashid pauses with a sneer. Clearly he doesn't agree with the pharaoh's taste. "He was Senenmut, the architect who later built her famous mortuary temple."

Senenmut! The name plummets deep inside of me, and I can hear the dream voice echo in my ears again. "Find him!" I'm awake now, not dreaming, but the voice is clear. I'm suddenly absolutely dead certain that the "him" I'm supposed to find is Senenmut. Which makes no sense at all—how can I search for someone who died thousands of years ago? At least, I reassure myself, that means the voice and its demands have nothing to do with my mother. Whatever ghost I'm dealing with, it isn't hers.

The obelisks waver before my eyes, and for a brief minute I can hear them creaking against the ropes that raise them up. I see them wobbling, threatening to crash down on the army of men straining on the ropes before they settle into place. I let out the breath I didn't realize I'd been holding. It's done. The monuments to Hatshepsut's power stand for all time to admire.

"Senenmut? Sounds familiar—isn't there an action figure or a superhero with that name? Maybe it was a comic book. Anyway, what are you staring at for so long?" Adom grabs my elbow and yanks. "You said you wanted to see this place, so let's see it!"

"Okay, okay, now who's in a hurry?" I'm annoyed at Adom—he's always poking or grabbing me at the worst times. Either I'm trying to sleep or trying to concentrate. I blink, trying to recapture the scene I just imagined. But it's gone now. The obelisks still stand, weathered with the ages. They hold the rooted calm of ancient rocks that haven't shifted for many, many years. The teetering moment of rising, gleaming in the early morning sun, is replaced by the frenetic energy of a ten-year-old boy hopping from one foot to the other. I sigh and take Adom's hand, letting him drag me over to Rashid.

Our guide strides ahead into a courtyard flanked by papyrus-topped columns and massive statues that, he explains, represent the god Osiris, holding the scepter and the flail crossed over his chest and wearing the double crown of Upper and Lower Egypt, all symbols of the pharaoh. I stop to draw, hoping Adom and Rashid will go ahead and leave me alone in this amazing place.

"This is like something out of an Indiana Jones movie!" Adom squeals with excitement.

That's not what Rashid wants to hear. He seems

determined to replace Hollywood stereotypes with history, and he launches into a long description of the Osiris myth, religious architecture, and the role of priests in ancient Egyptian culture. As Adom circles the columns, reading the hieroglyphs with his own invented interpretations along with the scraps that Dad's taught him, Rashid follows him, correcting and explaining like a private tutor.

Adom insists his reading of hieroglyphs is right because he's a whiz at rebuses and aren't hieroglyphics the same thing basically, word pictures? Plus, he's positive he remembers all the symbols Dad's quizzed him on, like a mountain meaning "far away" or "foreigner" and wavy lines standing for water. The two of them are so involved in correcting each other, I slip away unnoticed. I walk through a series of courtyards, each one narrower than the preceding one, letting my feet lead me the way I did in the Cairo museum. I turn a corner and am drawn to a small sanctuary carved from the same pink granite as the obelisks. A placard in the corner explains that the shrine, called the Red Chapel, was built by Hatshepsut.

I've been led to Hatshepsut again. Why do I feel compelled to look for monuments built by the woman pharaoh? I've traveled to lots of places, but this kind of thing has never happened to me before. I don't know what to make of it, but I'm here, so I scan the hieroglyphs covering the chapel. Too bad I can't decipher hieroglyphs as well as Adom. He has a much better memory when it comes to word pictures, probably from all the comics he reads. All I know is that when symbols are surrounded by an oblong box—a cartouche—it indicates a name. There are many names set apart by cartouches on this wall, but one is repeated more than any other. It shows a circle, a seated figure with a feather coming out of its head, and upraised arms. I copy it out carefully.

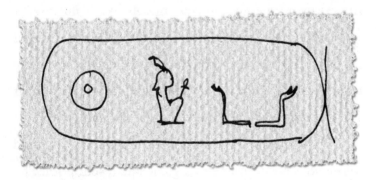

The sequence repeats itself over and over again—a circle, a seated figure, upraised arms. Sometimes the hieroglyphs are lined up horizontally, sometimes piled one on top of the other, but always in the same order, always the same symbols. I study the hieroglyphs, trying to figure out some pattern, some meaning to the ancient images, when one of the animal-headed figures bordering the cartouche suddenly moves. At least seeing it from the corner of my eye, I think it moved. I look again, coming closer. A falcon-headed god, Horus, stands next to the familiar name cartouche. I'm staring right at it when the profiled beak turns to me and speaks.

"Maat-ka-re," it says. "Maat-ka-re."

I can't be imagining this.

"Maat-ka-re. She is here." Then the falcon turns flat against the wall again, once more frozen in stone.

"I'm going crazy. This can't be jet lag. Or a weird virus. I'm even mumbling to myself like a nutcase." I back away from the shrine, afraid that if I take my eyes off of it, the carvings will start moving and speaking again. I edge behind a column, then turn and run. It doesn't matter where I go so long as it's away.

My heart is racing as I hurry through courtyards and colonnades until I come to a great square-cut pool. The water is low now, but I can see that at its original height, it would have mirrored the colossal statues of Osiris. Even the golden tips of the obelisks would have been reflected in the water's surface. It would have been a magical place then, not a swampy green marsh like now. I sit on a broken column and catch my breath, trying to sort through what I saw and heard: "Maat-ka-re." And "She is here." Who is she? And what does *Maat-ka-re* mean? The word is familiar. I'm sure I've heard it before, but I can't remember when or what it referred to. For once, I actually want to find Rashid and listen to him lecture. He may be creepy, but at least he's human—I know how to deal with him. I don't have a clue how I'm supposed to handle these voices, and it's beyond creepy for sculptures to move and talk.

The sun is low in the sky by the time Adom finds me sitting alongside the pool.

"We've been looking all over for you!" He slaps his thigh in exasperation, imitating a gesture of Dad's that seems ridiculous in a ten-year-old. "You've been here the whole time? What for? There's nothing to look at."

I stand up and shake out my legs, stiff from sitting on the cold stone for so long. "I was tired. I needed to sit and think."

"Perhaps it is time to go back to the hotel," suggests Rashid, coming up behind Adom. "It has been a long day. Tomorrow we can see the temple at Luxor."

Now that Rashid is here, I can't bring myself to ask him anything about the name on the chapel. The words won't come out. I let him usher me through the ruins, back through the courtyards, the high walls, to the avenue of sphinxes again. He holds my elbow firmly the whole time, as if I'm going to get lost again. But I wasn't lost in the first place and my skin burns where his fingers press in.

"I knew where I was," I protest. "I figured you guys would come that way eventually and then we'd all go home. Which is just what happened."

"Yes, of course." Rashid nods but keeps the pressure firm around my arm. "But I am responsible for you. Your father would never forgive me if something should happen. After all, to him, you are worth more than all of King Tut's treasure."

There isn't anything else to say. Even Adom is too tired to chatter. By the time we get back to the hotel, we're hungry, thirsty, and cranky as well as exhausted.

"It's all your fault, Talibah," Adom snaps. "If you hadn't gotten lost, we would have been here an hour ago!"

"Does it matter?" asks Rashid. "We are here now. Rest for a bit, then meet me in the dining room at seven. Once you have cleaned up and had a chance to relax, you will be as good as new, the both of you."

I try to make Adom feel better. I know that once he passes a certain point of irritated exhaustion, all hope for peace is gone—he's trapped in a spiral of crankiness that won't end until he drifts off to sleep. I offer him the first shower, but that doesn't appease him, so I give him the TV remote. That works. He's back to his cheerful self, wide-eyed in front of Cartoon Network. The hotel doesn't have a garden, but it does have cable and that's all that matters. Now that Adom's forgiven me, I'm eager to look at the book on Hatshepsut that Rashid gave me. Maybe I'll find answers to my questions in its pages.

Trying to block out the high-pitched noise of the cartoons, I read the short section on the temple at Karnak. I don't find much that's useful, but looking through the photographs in the book, I recognize the name cartouche I saw earlier—the circle, the seated figure, and the raised arms. The caption explains that it spells out Maatkare, Hatshepsut's chosen pharaoh name.

"Maat-ka-re." I read the name out loud. It feels powerful to me, even sitting in a modern hotel room. That's what the falcon god was telling me—the name is Hatshepsut's and she is there, or at least her name is. But I read on the placard that she had built the chapel, so of course her name would be on it. The hieroglyphs probably describe her great qualities, achievements, and gifts to her kingdom. I'm still puzzled. Why would the falcon hieroglyph insist that I notice the pharaoh's name? The more I learn, the less I understand. I quickly skim through the book, trying to read as much as possible before we have to go to dinner. The TV noise doesn't help my concentration, but I manage to get at least an overall sense of the woman pharaoh and the major features of her reign.

Hatshepsut seemed to be constantly justifying her right to rule, depicting herself as a man on her monuments. Considering average ancient Egyptians never actually saw their pharaohs, only the temples they built, this would be effective propaganda. Basically, Hatshepsut became ruler after the death of her husband, Thutmose II. Thutmose himself wasn't of royal blood and had gained the right to rule by marrying Hatshepsut, the previous pharaoh's royal daughter. The two of them had no sons, only a daughter. Thutmose II had a mistress of common blood like himself, and he had a son with her, Thutmose III. When Thutmose II died during his brief reign, Thutmose III was still very young, so Hatshepsut assumed the throne. First she ruled as guardian for her stepson, but as she grew into the role of leader, she took the title of pharaoh as well as the power. That's when she gave herself the name Maatkare, Keeper of Justice or Order. Even the name she chose showed that she was justifying her rule, insisting on its rightness. It seemed like the stereotypical evil stepmother story—the greedy, ruthless guardian stealing away the child's right to rule. But Hatshepsut was a popular and powerful pharaoh, something she couldn't have been without support from the priests and nobles. And she was royal, while her stepson wasn't. Even once Thutmose III reached adulthood, he left the running of the kingdom to his capable stepmother. He seemed content to wait until her death to begin his own regime. I add the family tree to my sketchbook, noting who was of royal blood, who was a commoner.

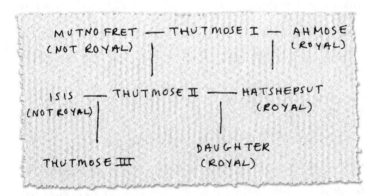

It was a complicated soap opera, especially since the ancient Egyptians had the confusing habit of marrying sisters to brothers or half-sisters to half-brothers to keep the power in family hands. The names didn't help me keep things straight, either. Hatshepsut's father, husband, and stepson were all named Thutmose, numbers one through three. Couldn't they have slipped a Ramses in there somewhere, or a Seti, simpler names to remember? I'm trying to figure out when exactly Hatshepsut decided to wear the pharaoh's crown when Adom jumps on the bed in front of me, bouncing the book out of my hands.

"Hey!" I squawk.

"Dinnertime!" Adom yells, jumping up and down like he always does on hotel beds—something he isn't allowed to do at home.

"I don't think so," I say, grabbing one of his slender ankles and pulling him down. "It's tickle time!" Adom erupts in squeals of laughter as I feather my fingers in his armpits and along his chest.

"Okay, enough," I say, laughing myself. "Let's eat. I'm starving!"

"Me too," Adom agrees, still panting.

We walk into the dining room, not surprised to find Rashid already sitting at a table in the corner. He looks up and waves us over.

Over a feast of fresh pita, hummus, tomato salad, and grilled chicken, Rashid explains more of the history of

Karnak. I wonder what he talks about when he's not lecturing, if he has a different personality when he isn't in professor mode. But for all he says, he doesn't tell me what I want to know. At least I don't need to ask him about the name cartouche since I found the answer in the book, but I still haven't learned much about the woman pharaoh's life. Or about Senenmut, the man in charge of the obelisks. And for some reason, I can't bring myself to ask Rashid anything.

As Dad's friend gestures with his fork or helps himself to pita, his heavy ring keeps catching my eye. I don't believe in the mummy's curse, but I wonder what it is about the ring that makes me distrust Rashid so much. For a second I'm reminded of the cobra, its cruel head swaying rhythmically, its split tongue flicking out of its mouth. That's ridiculous, I tell myself. He's a man, not a snake. But there's that dim similarity again, something about the eyes, maybe. Something I can't shake.

Another Page
from the Past

THE NEXT MORNING ADOM GOES ON STRIKE.
He refuses to go to any temples, tombs, monuments, or museums.

"This is my vacation, too!" he insists, glaring at the glass of orange juice in front of him. "I want to do something fun today."

"Like what?" I ask. "Go to a video arcade and have pizza for lunch? Where do you think we are, back in New York? I thought you wanted to go to that tomb."

"That cannot be for today," Rashid abruptly interjects. "I have arranged for that later this week. Do not worry." He pats Adom's arm. "You will go. And today you will have fun. How about a ride on a felucca, one of those little boats that skim the Nile? Then later we can go to the bazaar. Everyone likes the wonders of the market! You will see more snakes, maybe even a camel or two."

"Great!" Adom says.

I roll my eyes. "More snakes? Not for me, thanks."

Rashid looks surprised. "But I thought all young ladies like to shop. The bazaar does not interest you?"

"Uh, nooooo," I drawl, thinking, Not with you, no way, even though I really want to see the bazaar. Going to the tombs or temples, I feel dependent on Rashid, but shopping—that's definitely something I can manage on my own. I wish I could go alone with Adom, but since I can't, I'll figure out something else to do. I think of the book Rashid gave me and suddenly I know exactly how I want to spend my time.

"But how can you stay here at the hotel all day?" Rashid lifts his palms, puzzled, when I tell him. "What will you do?"

"Actually, I was hoping to find a library. That book you gave me got me interested in some historical stuff." I try to keep my voice as light as possible. "I'd like to do some research."

The corners of Rashid's lips curve up, like his face is ordering his mouth to smile. "Now that I can help you with! I can give you an introduction to the archeologists' library so that you will be permitted to use it. I'm sure you will find whatever you are looking for there." He looks around the table, so satisfied he reminds me of a boa constrictor that has swallowed a pig. There really is something serpentine about this man, and I feel a pang about leaving Adom alone with him.

But that lasts only a second—I know I'm being ridiculous. Adom will be fine, more than fine; he'll be happy. And so will I.

The Archeological Society Research Library is a lot like the rumpled Cairo museum. Instead of neatly organized books and gleaming computer terminals, the library Rashid leads me to is a labyrinth of dusty shelves; rusted filing cabinets; and piles of books massed on tables, chairs, and the floor. Even my small school library is in better shape. In fact, the janitor's closet there is more organized.

I look around in despair. "How do you find what you're looking for?" I ask.

"If you're doing research on dust, mold, and dirt, it'll be easy," Adom jokes.

"If you prefer, you can always come with us," Rashid

says, clearly offended that his generous offer of library privileges isn't being fully appreciated. I shouldn't criticize his gift, even though it's covered in giant dust bunnies.

So of course I tell him I'll be fine right where I am, surrounded by cobwebs with no computer catalog in sight, not even another person, except the woman in the atrium who signed me in.

"One of the great joys of research is the accidental discovery." Rashid gestures toward the shelves crammed with books and files, some upright, others askew, nothing looking like it's in its proper place. "It is often while you are looking for something else entirely that you make the most amazing finds."

"It's cool that this whole country doesn't believe in vacuuming or dusting," says Adom. "That's the discovery I made."

"Okay, now go discover something at the bazaar," I tease. "Maybe a gift for your beloved sister?"

"Yes, we will go now," Rashid agrees, leading Adom back to the door. "Remember to sign out at the front desk if you decide to walk back to the hotel before we drop by. Otherwise, we will pick you up in, say"— Rashid glances at his watch —"two, three hours."

I watch the door close behind them, relieved to be alone, even if this isn't the warm, comfortable library I'd imagined. I try to think of this place as an excavation site—my job is to dig through the rubble of books to find something on Hatshepsut or Senenmut. I have to start somewhere, so I approach one teetering tower of books and read the titles on the spines. Some are written in German, French, or Arabic. The ones in English seem just as foreign: *Notes on the Somatology and Pathology of Ancient Egypt, The Theocracy of Amarna and the Doctrine of Ba, The Hekanakhte Papers and Other Early Middle Kingdom Documents.*

I have to laugh at that last title—is there a Middle Middle Kingdom, a Late Middle Kingdom, a Middle Early Kingdom, and a Late Early Kingdom to go with the Early Middle one? I mean, how confusing can you get? What gave me the idea I would understand any of these books? I'm beginning to think the only thing I'll discover is how dense the English language can be.

Why can't they write in plain sentences? I think of how Mr. Harris, my English teacher, is always telling us to write clear, clean sentences. He says that the whole point of writing is to present a thought in a form that anyone can understand. If you don't get your point across, if it doesn't make sense, then it's bad writing, whether it's grammatically correct or not. I used to think that was pretty obvious and Mr. Harris was wasting his breath saying that kind of thing. Now I wish the people who wrote these books had taken classes with Mr. Harris!

I walk down one of the narrow corridors lined with shelves on either side, and I try to figure out if there's any kind of order to the books; it's a complete mix of titles, from magic to death rites to flora and fauna to architectural studies. The dust is so thick, it looks like none of the books have been touched in years. Only those piled on the tables in the main room seem more recently used.

As I scan the spines of the books, I notice that one book is teetering on the edge of the shelf, as if someone pulled out the one next to it and left its neighbor sticking out dangerously by mistake. I reach over to push it back in so it won't fall, but the title on the spine catches my eye, *Daughters of Isis: Women of Ancient Egypt*. It sounds like what I'm looking for. And it's in plain English, an extra bonus.

I turn to the table of contents, and I'm not surprised to see that there's a brief chapter on "The Woman Pharaoh, Maatkare." Most of the information is the same as what I read in the book Rashid gave me, but I'm excited to see there are also a couple of paragraphs on Senenmut.

"The enigmatic 'Steward of Amen,'" I read,

Senenmut stands out as being the most important and able administrator of this period. Originally a man of low birth who started his career in the army, Senenmut remained a bachelor and devoted his life to Hatshepsut's service. His precise relationship with the queen is unclear, although he seems to have been accorded unusual privileges for a non-royal male and it is difficult to determine exactly how much of his meteoric rise to prominence was due to his personal relationship with the widowed queen.

So he wasn't just the pharaoh's architect. He wasn't simply in charge of monuments. He ran the kingdom with Hatshepsut. He was her partner, probably in more ways than one, since he never married. In one of his many lectures about family responsibility, Dad's told me about the importance of family to the ancient Egyptians—everyone got married unless there was something really wrong with them. It would have been very unusual for a man to stay single, especially one of such position, wealth, and power. But of course, Senenmut, being of low birth, couldn't have married the pharaoh, much as they might have loved each other. And if he'd been of high birth, she might not have married him anyway, since that would have meant losing her power over the throne. Hatshepsut reminds me of Queen Elizabeth I, who ruled in sixteenth-century England, because her father, Henry VIII, left no male heir except for a sickly boy who died soon after his famous father. Elizabeth talked about marrying a Spanish or French noble, but she decided she loved her country more than any man, and while she took lovers, like the notorious Earl of Essex, she remained "the Virgin Queen." And she turned out to be one of the best rulers England ever had, strengthening and expanding her empire as well as fostering an explosion of creativity. I smile, imagining Hatshepsut as an Egyptian Queen Elizabeth—proud, intelligent, gifted at politics and empire building. When I think of her that way, she seems more like a real human being and less like a stiff granite sculpture. I draw her next to Elizabeth. They seem a good match.

Was Senenmut Hatshepsut's lover? I think of the voice again, its urgent plea to "Find him!" Now the tone makes sense to me—the insistent drive, the naked need behind the words. Hatshepsut—or her spirit—is searching for her lover. But how was he lost?

The book goes on to describe how Senenmut built two costly tombs for himself, but that he was never buried in either one, perhaps because he fell out of favor. His name disappeared from the historical record during Hatshepsut's reign, and after his death, reliefs and statues of him were defaced and his tomb was desecrated.

I'm wondering why Senenmut had two tombs, and the book answers my question. He built the first one in the Valley of the Nobles, before becoming a close confidant to the pharaoh. His second tomb, the splendid, unfinished one, was built directly under Hatshepsut's temple, the one I still haven't seen. I'm not an Egyptologist, but I know that it wouldn't be normal for a commoner to have a tomb so close to the temple of a mighty pharaoh. It seems like another clue showing how intimately Senenmut and Hatshepsut were connected, both in life and death.

Except if he wasn't buried in either of the tombs he built, not the first one or the second, fancier one, I wonder what happened to his body. The book is maddeningly silent on the question. Am I supposed to search for a mummy? And what really happened to Senenmut? Did he fall from favor, get banished even? Or simply die? And why would his images and name cartouches be vandalized? What was he being punished for? Maybe he was more like the Earl of Essex than I imagined—maybe he was a traitor against his queen-lover and was executed like the British earl was. But wouldn't there be some kind of historical record of his treachery, some clue to why he was dishonored?

If this was a soap opera, Senenmut would have cheated on Hatshepsut, and she would have gotten so angry that she would have exiled him and then tried to erase his memory from the land.

Maybe it was a soap opera—maybe that *was* what happened. And that's why he's lost—he was sent out of Egypt and now Hatshepsut's spirit can't rest until she knows what happened to him. But if that's true, how do I find out where he ended up? I turn back to the book, hoping for some sort of guidance.

The rest of the short chapter describes the major achievements under Hatshepsut's long rule and the succession by her stepson. There's no more mention of Senenmut, but the last paragraph catches my attention:

Signs of her reign were destroyed after her death . . . Her portraits and cartouches were defaced and her monuments were either destroyed or re-named.

Once again I can hear the falcon-headed god rasp out, "Maat-ka-re. She is here." And she is! Hatshepsut's pharaonic name is all over the Red Chapel. She hasn't been erased from there, from one of the central shrines in the holiest temple of the kingdom. In the heart of Egypt, her name still lives.

Then why was it erased elsewhere, I wonder. And were Hatshepsut's monuments defaced at the same time as Senenmut's? Was there a link between the two? I understand less than ever, though one thing is clear—the pharaoh and her architect are intimately connected. It's a union that outlived death, outlasted the millennia. And somehow I'm in the center of it all, charged with bringing the two lovers back together again.

7

Hidden Treasure

I'VE SPENT BARELY AN HOUR IN THE LIBRARY, but I'm not sure I have the energy to search for any other books. Still, I don't know when I'll have another chance to rummage through the shelves, and so many questions remain unanswered. I pace slowly down one corridor and up the next, pausing to scan titles. I find an interesting book on black magic and a beautiful brocade-bound book on the art of mummification, but nothing else on either Hatshepsut or Senenmut.

I'm sliding a heavy leather-bound history of the pyramids back on the shelf when a shimmering light catches my eye and I notice a slender silver book wedged behind the others, flat against the wall. I shift the books that block it, thinking only to line it back up on the shelf spine-out, but as my fingers grasp it, I feel a strange tingling. Pulling it close I see there's no title, just a smooth cloth cover. When I open it, there's no title page either, just an explanation that what follows is the translation of a New Kingdom papyrus from the time of Hatshepsut.

Hatshepsut again. I'm not even surprised. I'm expecting her name now. Still, I can't believe I'm holding in my hands words that were written nearly 3,500 years ago! Even in translation, I feel the weight of their enormous age. Who could have written it? What can it tell me about Hatshepsut and Senenmut?

The pages look like they're ready to fall out, so I hold the book carefully and take it back to the first room, clear a space at one of the tables, and sit down to read. As I open it, I catch a whiff of incense, of sun-baked sand. It's the same smell as the old woman, the one who gave me the carving. I'm beginning to recognize it as the smell of ancient Egypt.

"Scribe, I remind myself. I am Meru the scribe," the book begins.

I am practiced in writing, expert in drawing, the reed pen like the fingers on my hand. Still I find this daunting, to invent words to put on papyrus instead of simply copying what is before me or what is said. But Senenmut has encouraged me to compose my own writing. "You can write imaginary adventures or you can write what you see here, living in the palace of Egypt's greatest pharaoh, Maatkare. You could even set down my life, perhaps better than I can do, and your words will grace the walls of my tomb."

I feel like a heavy door has opened and I've been invited into Meru's world, the world of Senenmut and Hatshepsut. I see through Meru's eyes, hear through his ears. His words draw me in to a time thousands of years ago.

So I will write down Senenmut's life as I see it. My own life is a blank papyrus waiting for a story, but his is truly a life worth recording for generations to read about, even if my words are thin and weak compared to his vigor and keen mind. For where he is like a lion, I am like a cat. Where his thoughts are quick and graceful like a gazelle, mine are slow and plodding like a river horse.

I stop reading again, stunned by what I'm holding in my hands—a translated document about Senenmut's life written while he still lived! It's more than a rare find, it's something I didn't imagine could survive the ages. It even has drawings in it, a hippo and antelopes that I copy into my sketchbook.

As I read, I can see the oil lamp flickering on the table where the boy, Meru, wrote. I can hear the scratch of the reed pen against the papyrus. I can smell incense burning in a shallow bowl in the corner of the dark room. As I follow the words on the page, I hear Senenmut's voice as he describes cutting the great obelisks and directing their placement. It's the same scene I imagined when I was standing there at Karnak, watching the obelisks rise into the sky until their tips pierce the blue and they stand straight and tall.

Meru even mentions the high priest, the official whose tomb Rashid is excavating. My skin prickles as I read the description:

Hapuseneb is from an old priestly family. He is supreme judge of the land as well as Great Priest of Amon. His power, both political and religious, is enormous, but still not as great as Senenmut's. Where Senenmut is gracious and charming, his wit shining like the golden obelisks, Hapuseneb is sour and angry, his face set in a perpetual scowl. He is like a lump of Nile mud next to Senenmut's gleaming brilliance, which only makes him more resentful of Senenmut's high position.

Unfortunately, Meru works under the priest's direction on the tomb being prepared for the pharaoh—for Hatshepsut. Though he doesn't like the taskmaster, he clearly likes the work, giving elaborate recipes for mixing colors and listing the steps to prepare the wall's surface first for sketches, then carving, then painting. Now that I understand the work behind their creation, I'll never look at tomb paintings the same way. I'm so absorbed in Meru's world, I lose track of the time until the slam of the heavy front door reminds me where I am, both in time and space.

I look at my watch—are Adom and Rashid back already? I don't know when I'll be able to come back to the library, but I can't leave the book behind. I slip it carefully into my backpack—I'm not stealing, I tell myself, just borrowing. By the time Adom rushes into the room, disturbing several layers of dust, I've composed my face into a mask of calm, though my heart is pounding furiously.

"Look what I got for you!" Adom says, holding out a small wrapped parcel.

"You did get your sister a gift." I smile, firmly back in the present again. I really wasn't expecting anything, but of course, I'm glad he brought me something.

"Open it, come on, open it!" Adom hops from one foot to the other. He's as excited as if the surprise was for him, not from him.

"It's not a scorpion is it? Or a snake?" I tease.

"No! That would be wasted on you," Adom says, jumping around me.

Rashid walks into the room. "I have signed you out, so we can go now. Ah, I see Adom has given you his gift. He took a long time choosing, I should tell you. He selected this very carefully."

"Really?" I ask Adom. He nods, proud of himself. I untie the string and unfold the paper to uncover a silver bracelet with a carved blue scarab beetle mounted on it.

"Oh," I say, startled by such a treasure. Usually Adom gets me things that are in his taste, not mine, like earrings shaped like spiderwebs or charm bracelets with tiny baseballs and tennis rackets. This is different—I love it. It's even better than the snake bracelet the old woman wore. To me it feels just as old, just as powerful. "It's so beautiful!" I gasp.

"And it's magical, too! Look," Adom directs me. "The scarab hides a secret compartment. You press here to release the catch and . . ." He pivots the scarab back like a lid, revealing a small space big enough for a coin or a gem, but not much more. "Isn't that cool? And it looks really old, too. I bet it's an antique or something."

"Or simply needs cleaning," suggests Rashid. "But old or new, it is very nice. And scarabs had magical powers for the ancient Egyptians. They could protect you from the evil eye. It is a thoughtful present, Adom."

"Thank you." I hug my brother, wishing Rashid would disappear and leave the two of us alone. "It's perfect," I whisper in his ear. Aloud, I say, "And for yourself? What did you get?"

"This!" Adom points to the necklace around his neck. At the end of the silver chain hangs a tiny sarcophagus. "See, it opens up, too." Sure enough, a tinier silver mummy nestles inside, snug in its little case.

"Wow!" I'm impressed. Egypt has clearly improved my brother's taste in jewelry. "That was some bazaar."

"Ah, now you regret staying here," Rashid says. "Well, tomorrow you will come with us. We will cross the Nile to the western shore, where all the tombs and funerary temples are. So you will still get a boat ride. And perhaps we can visit the bazaar again another day."

"Okay," I agree. Even with Rashid, the bazaar definitely seems worth visiting. "But I did like the library. I found some interesting books."

I stop to thank the woman at the front desk as we leave.

"Come again, whenever you like." She smiles at me, then turns back to the files on her desk. There's a flash of gold on her wrist. I lean over for a closer look and recognize the same snake bracelet that the old woman wore. I gasp. Is it a coincidence? What does it mean?

"Is something wrong?" Rashid gives me one of his too-intent looks, the kind that makes me want to pull on a baggy sweatshirt and hide my face in its hood.

"No, nothing," I murmur. "I'm just thinking about the books I read."

"You must tell me about them." Rashid smiles.

That's the last thing I want to do, but I'm pinned by his gaze and can't say anything.

"Can we go now?" Adom tugs at my sleeve. "I'm hungry! When are we going to have lunch?"

"Of course, lunch!" Rashid turns back to the door. "I know just the place. Come, come. We can talk about your books while we eat."

"Sure," I mutter, but I'm determined not to tell Rashid anything. If he insists, I'll mention the history of the pyramids or the book on magic. After all, I glanced at those. The silver book hidden in my backpack has to be kept secret. I take one last look at the woman as we leave, but she's not behind her desk anymore. She's vanished among the shelves. I touch the scarab on the bracelet, wondering if it will really protect me from the evil eye, although right now the only eye I want to ward off is Rashid's.

X

The Wrong Name

AFTER LUNCH, ADOM WANTS TO PLAY IN the pool. Rashid quickly agrees that it's a great idea, especially since he has work he needs to do without pesky kids trailing after him. He doesn't actually say the part about us being annoying pests, but I can tell he's relieved to be rid of us for the afternoon. As he walks away, I'm tempted to stick out my tongue, because the feeling is definitely mutual—I'm thrilled not to have him anywhere near us for the rest of the day.

I take my backpack with me to the pool, and while Adom splashes around in the shallow end, I plunge back into the silver book from the library. Even in the bright glare of the afternoon sun, just holding it in my hands makes me feel transported into a different world. As I read, I feel like I can finally see the mysterious Senenmut.

There is an intensity in Senenmut's eyes so that when he looks at you, you feel you are the most important person in the world, bathed in the warmth of his gaze. But if he is angry and flinty, those same eyes can crush you with the weight of his scorn or sear you with the heat of his rage.

I know that is how Neferure feels too, longing for a kind look from Senenmut. I see it in how she follows him, how she wants always to be close to him.

I don't know who Neferure is. I don't remember hearing the name before, but as I read it, a stabbing pain shoots through me, blooming into a ragged gouge deep inside me. My eyes well up with tears and I'm shaken by sobs, my whole body racked with an intense grief. I haven't felt this way since Mom died, and I don't know why Neferure's name should conjure up such sorrow now, except that Mom's name started with an N, too—Naima.

"Naima!" I stop crying long enough to blurt out her name. It sounds strange. I realize I haven't heard anyone say it in years. "Naima," I call again, but it's not really what I want to say. "Mama!" I sob. That's it, the word I haven't spoken in five years. I abandon myself to the tears, my whole body shuddering.

I'm hunched over like that, sobbing, when I notice cold water dripping on my bare feet. Then a damp, chilled hand touches my shoulder. I look up and see Adom staring at me, his face tight with worry.

"What's the matter?" he asks. "What happened?"

I gulp down air to calm myself and wipe the wet off my face. "Nothing, I'm fine." I try to smile. "It's just the book I'm reading. It's very sad."

Adom's brow furrows. "I didn't know a book could *be* that sad."

Now I really do smile. Adom smiles, too, relieved I'm not crying anymore.

"Maybe you should read something else," he offers. "I'm almost finished with my comic book. Why don't you try that? It's not sad at all."

I wipe my nose on a corner of the towel I'm sitting on. "I'm okay. It's a sad book, but it's interesting. I want to know how it ends."

When I've convinced Adom that I really am fine, he gets back into the water, but I notice he keeps an eye on me. He splashes around, then pauses to check on me to make sure I haven't dissolved into tears again. I wave and smile at him. Who's supposed to be taking care of whom, I wonder.

Now that I'm calm, I can think about Neferure. I don't know why her name sparked such a strong reaction in me, and I'm not sure it matters. What's important is the story of Senenmut and what place Neferure had in his life. I pick up the book and start reading again.

Neferure is Hatshepsut's daughter by the Pharoah Thutmose II. Senenmut was her tutor when she was young, and, like her mother, she adores him. She calls him "Wise One" and "Charmer of River Horses," saying he is so sweet with words that even the vicious beasts obey him. And to her, he is sweet, as loving as if she were his own daughter. When she was little, Senenmut would take Neferure hunting with him. He showed her how to use the throwstick to strike a duck as patiently as if he were training a young prince, not a girl. But a girl is not a prince, even if her mother is a pharaoh when women aren't

pharaohs. Maatkare is an exception chosen by the
gods. Without her, there would have been no one of
royal blood to rule. Neferure will sit on a throne too,
but only as queen, as a pharaoh's wife. She is soon
to marry Thutmose III, her younger half-brother.

It's hard for me to keep all the Thutmoses straight. I
sketch out a family tree in my journal. Neferure is the
child of Hatshepsut and Thutmose II. Thutmose III is the
child of Thutmose II and his common mistress. Neferure
is the one with the royal blood, but Thutmose III is
the one who'll become pharaoh. He gains the position
because of his father and stepmother and because he'll
marry into the royal bloodline with Neferure. All their
children will be royal because of her, not him. I draw
another family tree, this time with Neferure.

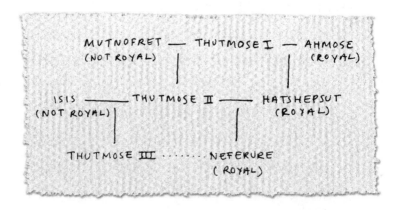

What about Senenmut? Thutmose II dies and Hatshepsut takes over as pharaoh, while raising her stepson to succeed her on the throne and grooming her daughter to marry her stepson. Along with all his other important titles, she puts Senenmut in charge of Neferure's education. She makes him, in effect, a kind of father to her daughter. Is he also, I wonder again, the pharaoh's lover? He has so many intimate ties with the royal family, why not that one as well?

I wish Meru would write about that! Instead he continues with a description of Thutmose III, who is already a young warrior, old enough to rule, but content to follow his stepmother's orders.

I tremble whenever I see Thutmose III. He is proud and fierce and carries himself grandly, with splendidly coiled muscles ready to charge, just like Ankhu, the pet lion who goes everywhere with him. If Neferure loves Senenmut, Thutmose III clearly does not. Like the vizier Hapuseneb, he thinks my uncle wields more power than he should rightly have. So when he heard that Senenmut wanted to delay his marriage to Neferure, Thutmose was enraged, snorting like an angry bull. He even started rumors that Senenmut planned to wed Neferure himself!

This really is a soap opera! Could it get any more complicated and intertwined? Could Senenmut be Hatshepsut's lover but plan to marry her daughter, since the mother wants to share her bed with him but not her throne? That would be a good reason for Hatshepsut to send Senenmut into exile. Maybe that's what happened—the pharaoh's jealous rage was directed not just at any other woman, but at her own daughter!

I draw hearts on my family chart connecting Senenmut with Hatshepsut, then more hearts linking the tutor to his student and Neferure to her half brother. When I'm finished it's all a tangled mess with hearts and lines all over the place.

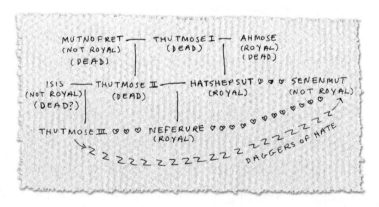

I'm about to pick up the book again when Adom gets out of the pool and flops down on the lounge chair next to me.

"I'm tired of swimming," he says. "I want to dry off in the sun, and then let's go back to the room."

"Okay," I agree. "I'll take a quick swim while you soak in the sun. Do you mind?"

"A short swim, not a zillion laps." Adom closes his eyes.

I jump into the pool and start swimming underwater, trying to make it to the other side without breathing. My muscles feel strong and efficient as I move. At least here, swimming, I feel in control, like I know what I'm doing.

Suddenly the water chills and darkens, like a cloud has covered the sun. I hear a thudding slam as if a very heavy door has been shut, and then a voice demands, "Neferure! Find him! Find him!" Even underwater, I recognize it as the voice from my dream! What is going on? I start to push up to the surface. "Neferure!" the voice hisses again. "Find him!" And then I break out of the water, gasping, and the voice is gone, the darkness vanished. I cling to the edge of the pool, trying to calm my breathing. I peer at the deep end, but there's no one else, nothing else in the pool except me.

It's all a big mistake. Whoever wants me to find Senenmut has picked the wrong person. I'm not Neferure, I'm just an innocent bystander. Somebody else was supposed to have the dream, somebody else was supposed to fall into the scene painted on the papyrus, to see the sphinx move. What about the stone carving—I wonder with a jolt—was somebody else supposed to get that, too? I clamber out of the pool, throw a towel around my goose-bumpy shoulders, and dig into my backpack. At first I think I've lost it or it's disappeared somehow, but then my fingers find it. I bring it out into the light and study the detailed structure. It's as beautiful and delicate as I remember. I want it to belong to me, not to be a mistake.

"That really was a short swim," Adom says. He sits up and touches the small carved building. "That is so cool! I haven't seen anything like it in the souvenir stalls around here. What do you think it's a model of?"

"Does it have to be a model of something? It doesn't look anything like the temples at Karnak and Luxor."

"I know, but it's a real place." Adom sounds certain. "It's just one we haven't seen yet."

I'm still freaked out by the voice in the pool, but I'm relieved that the miniature building is here in my hands and definitely mine, whether it's an imagined place or not. I tuck it carefully into my backpack and settle back into the lounge chair, picking up Meru's book. A scrap of paper flutters out from between the pages.

"What's this?" I ask, reaching for it. "How did it get here?"

"The old lady must have slipped it in," Adom says.

"What old lady? What do you mean?"

Adom shrugs. "Just some old lady. I thought she was a maid or something. She was tidying up stuff and she picked up your book, then put it back down. Believe me, I wouldn't have let her take it! It looked like she was cleaning up, that's all."

"Can you describe her, Adom? Think!" I have a weird feeling it's the same old woman who gave me the carving.

"I dunno. She was short, hunched over, and very wrinkly. Like your standard old lady. Nothing special about her." Adom pauses. "Except she smelled good. Usually old people are kind of musty. She smelled good, like spices."

I smile. It has to be her! "Did you notice if she was wearing a bracelet, a snake one?"

Adom scrunches his face in concentration. "I think

so. I don't remember a snake exactly, but there was definitely something shiny and golden on her wrist."

"Thanks, Adom, you're a genius!" I kiss him loudly on the cheeks. "It's the same woman who gave me the sculpture you like so much. She left me another gift!"

"A scrap of paper?" Adom frowns. "Not much compared to her first present."

"Depends what's on the paper—maybe it's a secret message! Let's see what it says." I place the paper on the table between us so we can both read it.

It's a hieroglyph in crisp black ink. The symbols are held inside an oblong box, which means it's a name, but whose? All I can tell is that it isn't Maatkare, Hatshepsut's royal name. Could it be Neferure's? I copy it into my sketchbook.

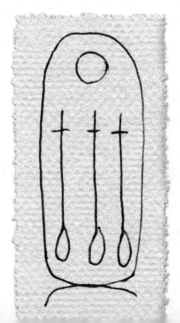

"You're the expert on hieroglyphs," I say to Adom. "It's a name, right? Do you recognize it?"

Adom shakes his head. "It could be a name or a title, like high priest or governor."

"How can you tell?" I'm impressed.

"I can't really." Adom looks at me. "That's what I think, but I can't promise. We could ask Rashid."

"No!" I snap. "We'll figure it out ourselves. Right now it's getting late. We should go back to the room before we catch a chill."

Adom's teeth are already chattering and he hugs his towel closer. "Dibs on the first shower!"

"You go ahead," I say. All I want to do is flop on the bed, turn on the TV, and turn off my brain. I put Meru's book, slip of paper included, into my backpack and collect our towels. I've had enough reading, enough of Meru's world for now. I need some time thinking of nothing at all.

9

Holy of Holies

I'M BOTH AFRAID TO READ MORE OF MERU'S book and afraid not to. I want to finish it, but I'm not sure I want to learn more about Neferure. She seems to be the one who's really being called to this task, not me.

It's too early to get up, but I can't go back to sleep. Adom is happily dreaming, but I'm staring up at the ceiling debating whether I should pick up the silver book or lose myself in the Stephen King paperback I brought. I reach for the novel but my fingers close on the silver cloth book, and before I know it I'm back in Meru's world.

Sometimes when he wants to unburden himself, Senenmut calls me to him and my task is to sit and listen, to open my heart to his words. "Hatshepsut says she has waited long enough for this marriage, any longer will cause ripples of discontent among the nobles and priests. Thutmose is already sixteen, Neferure eighteen." My uncle sighed. "She is right. And she is wrong. It is a path of shifting sands, difficult to follow, but she could wait one more year."

I do not ask why wait another year, although that is what I think. What difference can one more year make? Maatkare is a strong, established king. Thutmose is a headstrong youth. What chance does he have to grab the throne from her? And why should he? It will be his soon enough. The Pharaoh has already seen almost forty summers, a good, long lifetime. But what I think doesn't matter. I am there to listen, not to answer.

And it does not matter what Senenmut thinks, either. The Pharaoh knows her own mind, so now the Palace is humming with preparations for Neferure and Thutmose to wed. The priests are arranging elaborate sacrifices and feasts to celebrate the great union. All of Thebes vibrates with excitement. A festival means gifts of meat, beer, and bread to all the people. It means colorful processions, songs, and dances. It means a chance to approach the gods with wishes, hopes, and questions.

Meru doesn't describe himself, but I can see him sitting with his slender legs bent under him, leaning over the papyrus with his reed brush. His thin shoulders and chest are bare. He is young, only a little older than Adom, with large black eyes that try to penetrate the mysterious, powerful world of his uncle. I close my eyes and I can see Senenmut, too, a craggy lion of a man with full lips and piercing eyes. He is both intimidating and charming and I understand why he has such a strong hold over those who love him. I hold his image in my mind's eye, hoping to find the reason he disappeared, but there are no clues in the picture I've conjured up. Next I try to imagine Neferure. At first, all I can see is the back of her head, her long hair braided in rows. Then slowly she turns to face me, the haze around her clearing until I recognize her almond eyes and full lips. I'm seeing myself! My eyes fly open and the portrait vanishes. Are we connected because we look alike, or do I imagine us as sisters because I want that relationship? I've never thought about having a sister before—the person I miss is Mom, not some phantom sister. Do I really have a link to Neferure? Are these mental pictures real, delivered to me by Meru's words, or am I just daydreaming? It felt like a trance, but also very real. The book has a strange hold over me, its words weighted like a magic spell, but I can't understand how or why. I try to forget about Neferure, to focus only on Meru and what is happening to him. As I read, I see that there are drawings in this part of the book, so I copy them into my sketchbook.

I was working at the temple, finishing the scene where the Pharaoh sent an expedition to Punt, when Senenmut came near. I thought he would correct my drawing because I depicted the Queen of Punt as the sailors had described her, round and fat with chins layering on chins. She was so big that I felt sorry for the small donkey standing nearby that was charged with carrying her and I added a note next to the queen that the poor beast would be burdened with the queen's stomach. But Senenmut didn't criticize my sketches. Instead he drew me away, saying he wanted to speak to me privately. His eyes were moist and feverish with excitement and I thought he was inflamed because the wedding was planned, despite his objections, for the coming week. He was clearly distracted, but he paused to look at my work. When his eyes fell on the fat queen, a smile danced on his lips.

"Well done, Meru," he said. "Your art will allow generations to recall the glories of Maatkare's rule. But I want to show you something meant NOT to be seen or read by human eyes."

I could not guess what he meant. All the monuments Senenmut worked on were meant to be

admired for ages to come, by thousands yet unborn.
Then it flashed into my mind that he meant his
tomb—burial chambers were for the eyes of the
dead and the gods alone.

I knew that he had abandoned his original tomb
and tunneled a second one that lay precisely beneath
the inner shrine of Maatkare's Temple. When he
started the work, rumors raced around the court about
how inappropriate it was for a commoner to be buried
so near the Pharaoh's holiest shrine, in a direct line
beneath it. Nothing like it had been done before but
we all understood that it was a mark of the singular
favor the Pharaoh showed Senenmut. For them to be
linked so closely in the afterlife was a testament to the
strong bonds of their relationship in this one.

So I expected to be led down into the earth, down
the corridors to Senenmut's second tomb. Instead, my
uncle guided me to the top terrace of the temple, to
the shrine of the Pharaoh herself. I have not worked
on this part of the building so I have not seen these
innermost chambers, but clearly Senenmut had chosen
his best craftsmen for these walls. The drawing was
elegant and fluid, the colors rich and vibrant, but
that was not what my uncle wanted me to admire.

"Look," he whispered, closing the doors, leaving only the torchlight to see by. At first I didn't know what he wanted to show me. I only thought it strange that he closed the doors, shutting out the sun. Even the priests don't close the doors when they perform the sacred rites. The doors are barred only when the shrine is empty and not being used.

I gasped. That was what Senenmut had brought me to see. He wanted to show me what could only be seen from inside with the doors shut, what was clearly not meant ever to be looked upon by human eyes. There, carved on the walls on either side of the threshold—and normally hidden by the opened doors—were portraits of Senenmut himself.

"Yes." He *nodded*. "See! This way I will always be with the Pharaoh. I will be part of her cult, worshipping her along with the priests, until these walls crumble into dust."

I was too stunned to say anything. It was daring enough for Senenmut to connect his grave so closely to the Pharaoh's, but here he had put himself into the holiest of holy places. It was a shrine only for the Pharaoh, his queen (when the Pharaoh was a man, as was usually the case), and the gods. If Hapuseneb learned of such shocking vanity, he would surely demand Senenmut's removal from the Palace. He might even charge him with treason, with placing himself on the same level as the divine Pharaoh.

Why was my uncle showing me this? I covered my eyes. If this was sacrilege, I didn't want to know about it.

Senenmut chuckled. "Do not fear, Meru. You may uncover your eyes. I have done nothing without the Pharaoh's blessing."

"She knows?" The words rasped on my suddenly dry tongue.

Senenmut lifted his chin proudly and the shadow of his young, handsome self flitted across his old man's face. "Since we cannot be wed in this life, this is how we will be joined for all eternity. So is her desire, so is mine."

"Why show me?" I asked, trembling. "This is not for me to know."

"Perhaps," said Senenmut, "but I am so full of the Pharaoh's secrets, it is hard to hold my own. I must tell someone, and you are the one I most trust."

"What about the workers who carved this? What if they . . ." I couldn't bring myself to finish the thought. One word to Hapuseneb—it was too awful to contemplate.

Senenmut rocked back on his heels complacently. "No need to fear them. I left the carving of my name for last. That part I drew and painted myself and made sure the carver was a man who couldn't read. To him, my name was merely a series of shapes, nothing more."

That night my head swirled with horrible nightmares. Monsters devoured first my uncle, then me, while the high priest watched and laughed. Over and over again powerful teeth gnashed our bodies until right before dawn when the Pharaoh herself came and rescued my uncle, seating him on the throne beside her. I woke up hot and sweaty, my jaw aching from being clenched tightly all night. At last I understood why Senenmut had showed me, why it was so important to him now. It was because of the wedding. He was telling me that the Pharaoh still loved him best, even if she was giving her daughter to Thutmose, even if that gave her stepson more power, more even than Senenmut.

And I thought I had bad dreams! My own jaw tenses up as I read Meru's story. Now there's no question of what Senenmut was to Hatshepsut. They were certainly lovers or he never would have been granted the intimate connection Meru describes, but it was clearly a dangerous relationship, one that had to be hidden for Senenmut's own safety. What would Thutmose III have done if he had known? Or Hapuseneb? Perhaps one of them did find out and murdered Senenmut. Maybe it wasn't exile that tore him away from the pharaoh. Maybe it wasn't her doing that he disappeared, but someone else's. If Thutmose or the high priest killed the architect, then Hatshepsut might not have known what happened to him. He could have simply vanished one day, his body secretly buried or left to feed the vultures in the desert.

If that was true, how could I ever find Senenmut? Was I supposed to find out what happened to him rather than discovering his actual mummy? Is that what "Find him" means? The more I learn, the more questions I have. And maybe it's exactly those questions that the ghost needs answered. I'm relieved that I have more proof that the ghost isn't Mom. She wouldn't care about Senenmut. If she haunted anybody, it'd be Dad, to make him take better care of us, to make sure he told us stories about her instead of packing her away like an old photo album.

I'm about to dive back into the book when Adom bounces out of bed.

"Come on!" He tugs on my arm. "Look how late it is. We have to hurry to breakfast. Today Rashid's taking us across the Nile to the tombs and temples there, remember?"

"Of course I remember. Go wash up and we'll get ready to go." I slide the silver book into my backpack. As I get dressed, I notice the unopened Stephen King novel and think how funny it is that the ancient writing is as suspenseful to me as the modern book. I guess I do have a strange connection to ancient Egyptian things, like Dad says, and that's what makes them so powerful to me. Or maybe, I tell myself, it's just a fascinating story, a soap opera that anyone would find compelling.

My mind is full of Meru as we take the small boat with Rashid across the Nile to the west bank. Since the west is the direction of the setting sun, it's naturally the place for the dead and their worship, where all the mortuary temples and tombs are. It's where Meru would have lived and worked. I feel like I'm diving into the heart of the mystery now. I wish I could take this trip by myself, not that I mind Adom and his chatter, distracting as it is, but I don't want to be around Rashid. I don't care about the tour of the tomb he's excavating. Anything that has to do with Hapuseneb makes me shudder. And anything to do with Rashid doubles the goose bumps.

"You know," says Rashid, dipping his hand over the side of the boat into the Nile, "this river was once full of crocodiles." He grins at me, and for a second his mouth stretches wide, filled with sharp teeth, like he's a crocodile himself.

"What happened to them?" Adom peers into the murky water. I take his hand, reassured by his presence. He hasn't seen anything strange, so I must be imagining things.

"There are no longer enough fish for them to eat, so they have moved away." Rashid sighs. It sounds like a snake hissing. "Occasionally one shows up, but it is a rare sight. It was very sad to lose them."

"I'm glad they're gone," I say. "They give me the creeps."

"They do?" Rashid fixes me with his eyes. I feel like a butterfly pinned to a piece of cardboard. I can't help staring back at him, and as I watch, his brown eyes turn into yellow slits, rimmed by reptilian skin. I blink, but the crocodile eyes are still there, fixed in his face, staring into mine.

The boat jolts into the shore and the oarsman jumps out to tie it up. Rashid turns his sinister gaze away and steps out first. When he faces me again to offer a hand, his eyes are their normal soft brown. I shudder. There's no way I can touch him. I ignore his hand, teeter for a minute, then scramble safely out of the boat and reach back to help Adom out after me. Adom hasn't noticed anything—not the teeth, not the eyes, not the slithery voice. He doesn't hesitate to follow Rashid.

"Which tomb are we seeing first? The one you discovered?" Adom chatters. His excitement makes everything seem normal again. He slips his hand into mine and right away I feel better. "Is it near?" he asks. "Can we walk there or are we taking a camel?"

"Ugh," I say, wrinkling my nose. "No camels."

"What?" Rashid laughs. "You do not like Egyptian Cadillacs? They are the most comfortable way to travel in the desert. Sadly, however, we are taking a car. My driver is meeting us. Ah, there he is now." He points toward a battered old jeep.

Rashid introduces us to Ahmed, the driver, and we clamber into the car. As we drive into the desert, I forget about Rashid and the boat ride and a rush of excitement surges through me. This is the landscape I know from my dreams. We're closer than ever to Senenmut, to Meru, to the heart of their story.

Adom leans over the front seat and yells over the noise of the engine. "Are we going to the tomb you're excavating now? "

Rashid shakes his head. "Not yet. Tomorrow, I promise. Today there are other marvels to visit, and we will start with a temple—not a tomb—a mortuary temple."

"What's the difference between a mortuary temple and a regular one?" Adom asks.

"A mortuary temple is where the mummy of the dead pharaoh would be prepared and where, after the burial, the memory of the pharaoh would be celebrated. Tombs, remember, would be sealed and hidden after the mummy's burial because otherwise grave robbers would snatch all the treasures buried with the dead. So each pharaoh built his own mortuary temple and used it as a way of showcasing the achievements of his rule. The major battles and successes would be carved on the walls, and the innermost rooms would be sacred shrines for the cult of the pharaoh. The temple we are going to now is the most famous one of all. The architecture is like nothing that came before or after—it is truly a masterpiece, one of the wonders of the world. The quality of the painting and carving is superb, and the stories depicted offer fascinating insights into ancient Egyptian history, society, and religion."

I'm bored listening to Rashid, and I'm beginning to regret coming. He's either scary or dull, a strange combination of opposites. I thought we'd be going to tombs, not more temples. But as we turn away from the river toward the Theban mountains, I can't help gasping. The jeep pulls into a dirt parking lot and I climb out in a daze, mesmerized by the structure before us. It's exactly like the stone carving the old woman gave me— the three tiers, the ramps, the colonnades. It's all there, only vast in scale. I draw it in my sketchbook, my hand trembling. I can't believe I'm really here.

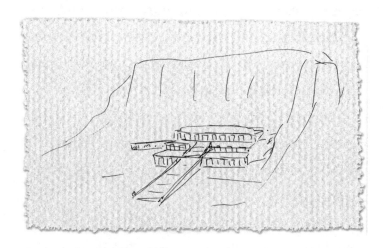

Adom jabs his elbow into my side. "See! I told you that thing's a model of something, and I was right! It's this! This is it!"

"Yes, you're right," I shush him. "Now be quiet about it—I don't want Rashid to know." Fortunately, Rashid's too distracted by the temple to pay attention to Adom's excitement.

Standing in front of the terraces, our guide opens his arms wide and starts explaining. "This is Deir El-Bahri, or the mortuary temple of Hatshepsut, Senenmut's architectural masterpiece. It was called the Holy of Holies when it was made."

I feel dizzy. This is the place Meru describes. This is where Senenmut's tomb is and where he dared to carve his likeness in the innermost shrine. And this is the place that the old woman thrust on me. Everything, everything comes back to Hatshepsut and Senenmut.

I try to focus on what Rashid is saying. I miss some of it, but he's explaining how originally the pharaoh had planned a tunnel connecting her temple to her tomb in the Valley of the Kings, the only kingly burial there for a woman.

"That is one reason why the back of the temple is carved out of the solid rock of the Theban mountains," Rashid lectures. "Unfortunately, the rock proved too hard for a tunnel to be feasible and the idea was abandoned. Still, the complex is an architectural marvel, seeming to grow out of the mountains themselves."

I nod, recalling Meru saying the same thing. I am walking where he walked, where they all walked. It's an odd sensation, as if time has stopped and the sand holds all our footprints at once. As I follow the path toward the lowest terrace, out of the corner of my eye I see a lush garden with trees on either side, but when I turn to face the green expanse head-on, all I see is sand and rubble. There is no garden, but I know there once was one.

Meru described it, along with the incense trees brought back from Punt.

"Stop here," Rashid commands, "and turn around to face the Nile."

Adom and I follow his instructions. We can barely make out the brown ribbon of the river at the horizon's edge.

"From here you can imagine the long road from the river's edge to where we now stand. It was lined on either side by sphinxes, figures with the body of a lion and the head of Hatshepsut. There would have been more than a hundred of these sphinxes! You can still see two of them in the museum in Cairo."

That was the sphinx that spoke to me! It once faced this road. I can see the twin rows of tawny lions, standing eternal guard on the god's path, shimmering like a mirage in the sun.

"Wow!" Adom gasps. "Too bad they aren't still here. That would look so cool! It would be a street of sphinxes like we saw at Luxor. Sphinxes were streetlamps or something to the ancient Egyptians, huh? They had them on the sides of all their roads."

"Not exactly." Rashid shakes his head. "Sphinxes were symbols of sacred power, used only for special routes.

They were for roads of the gods, not market streets. For example, the colossal sphinx marks the mortuary temple near the Giza pyramids, another holy place."

That reminds Adom of all the wonders he still hasn't seen here. "When are we going to go there? I want to see that sphinx and the pyramids. Can we go inside? Are mummies still there?"

"I am sure your father will take you, but right now we are here." Rashid leads us to the lowest terrace. Even though the building is nearly 3,500 years old, the remnants of bright colors still remain on some of the reliefs, especially on the ceiling, where yellow stars shimmer against a deep blue. Below them a row of cobras slither, blue heads held high over red-and-yellow bodies, and falcons spread their turquoise wings. The walls tell a story in pictures and hieroglyphics. I don't need Rashid to tell me what's happening. I recognize from Meru's description what is carved and painted before me. In layered bands, the artists show how the two great obelisks were quarried, mounted on boats, rowed down the Nile by an army of men, carried to the temple, and finally hoisted into place. Again I hear the creak of the ropes, see the straining muscles of the men pulling, watch the giant stone needles teetering before each one settles into its upright position. The scene has lost its color, but I can see the glint of the gold sheathing the obelisks. I can taste the dust kicked up by their movement. For a moment I have found Senenmut. He is here on this wall, proclaiming his proud achievement. But where does he go from here, I wonder. What happens next?

Adom is drawn to the battle scenes along the other side of the colonnade. "Look at all the spears poking into bodies and the chopped-off hands and heads! It's like a comic strip in stone."

"Yeah, the Sunday comics for ancient times," I say. "Or really more like Japanese manga or anime, where the story is always about good guys fighting bad guys."

Rashid frowns, not at all happy with the comparison. "This is history, not entertainment. Hatshepsut is recording her military successes. See, that is her, in the form of a sphinx, pouncing on her enemies."

I flinch. The fierce claws and powerful muscles remind me of the sphinx in the museum. I don't want to be the pharaoh's enemy. I don't want to be haunted by her, either, but I'm not sure I have a choice in the matter.

10

Scarred Stones

ADOM RACES UP THE RAMP TO THE MIDDLE terrace with Rashid hurrying after him. I don't know if our guide is worried about losing his charge or afraid Adom will touch something he shouldn't, but I'm grateful to be free of them both. I can feel the magic of this place, as if the stones are trying to tell me something. I reach into my backpack and take out the small carving. It feels odd to hold it out in the palm of my hand, the temple around us an echo of the exquisite miniature building. The temple contains itself now, like a small stone heart. As I walk up the ramp, the tiny columns seem to glow. I could swear the sculpture is throbbing in my hand like it did when the woman first gave it to me, pulsing with the soul of the Holy of Holies.

I close my hand over the carving and try to focus on the scenes sculpted onto the walls around me. There are tall trees, ships with men, thatched huts on stilts, and a fat woman striding heavily, rolls of fat jiggling on her arms and belly. It's as if the past and the present are folded together into the stone pictures before me, and I smile, recognizing the scene Meru described painting in his journal. I'm looking at his work and it's as fresh, as alive as the day he made it. I see the donkey and although I can't read the hieroglyphs next to it, I know what they say: "poor donkey who has the job of carrying such a fat woman." I know because Meru told me.

"Meru," I whisper to the images. "It's beautiful." I gingerly stroke the donkey's nose. I can hear my father's voice admonishing me not to harm the art—look with your eyes, not your hands, he always says. But I can't help it. I need to feel the stone that Meru's fingers shaped and colored. I can trace his presence in the contours, in the subtle dips and hollows drawn by his brush. I've already copied the fat queen of Punt from Meru's book, so now I sketch the donkey. I want to take this bit of Meru away with me.

I stare at the rest of the wall where men and animals are loaded onto the boats, heading back to Egypt. I follow their journey home to Thebes, walking slowly along the wall, keeping pace with the voyage. Then the story changes dramatically. A god stands before a queen. In the next scene there is a small naked boy, the divine child of the god and woman.

Adom jostles into me, pointing at the boy. "Look, he's like a miniature adult, not a boy. And he's not wearing any clothes!"

"Where did you come from? You shouldn't just run into people, you know." I tuck the carving into my backpack, afraid I'll drop it if Adom shoves into me again. "Rashid was explaining this stuff to me. You know what it is?" Adom doesn't wait for an answer, but rushes on, eager to show off his newly acquired expertise before Rashid reaches us and takes over the tour guide role. "This is the story of Hatshepsut's divine birth. See, she's trying to prove that her father was really the sun god, Amon-Ra, and that's why she's the pharaoh. It's like a giant propaganda poster from thousands of years ago."

"But the kid isn't a girl, it's a boy, so it can't be Hatshepsut," I point out the obvious. "That is definitely a boy."

Adom looks at me like I'm being especially dense. "Well, duh! But everyone knew that kings—pharaohs— were boys, *not* girls. So Hatshepsut was *showing* herself as a boy. Maybe she figured that years later, no one would remember she was really a woman and she would be just another king in a long line of kings. Or maybe she was arguing for why she should be pharaoh—she was the child of a god and *she* was really a *he*."

I roll my eyes. So now Hatshepsut wasn't the first woman pharaoh, she was the first transvestite king?

"What? You don't believe Rashid?" Adom gestures to our guide, who's catching up to us. "He's the one who told me. You act like I'm making all this up."

"No, I don't think that, and of course I believe Rashid." I try to smile at Dad's friend. "It just doesn't make sense for Hatshepsut to be a boy."

"Yes, it is unusual, but you must understand the scene in the context of all of Hatshepsut's sculpture." Rashid's voice is so loud, he's lecturing to everyone on the terrace. There are only a few scattered tourists. They turn their heads to listen, not embarrassed the way I am, but apparently grateful for the free lesson. "Early in her rule," Rashid continues, "Hatshepsut shows herself as a woman wearing the pharaoh's crowns. Then in her portraits, she begins to minimize her breasts and to dress in men's clothes until she looks entirely like a man. And here, of course, being naked, there is no question of her maleness. Did her subjects know that she was a woman? Probably. That was not the issue. More likely she was showing herself with the attributes of a pharaoh—the crowns, the scepters. All those were markings of a king. And being a man, wearing masculine clothes, those were also royal traits."

Adom nods. "See—I told you it was Hatshepsut!"

"But she didn't really dress like a man? She didn't pretend to be a man?" The idea is jarring. It doesn't fit with how I imagine Hatshepsut. I want her to be like Queen Elizabeth I, a proud, powerful woman, not a cross-dressing fake.

Rashid shrugs. "We have no evidence that she did.

Most likely she dressed like the woman she was. In her inscriptions, she uses both male and female forms for her names, so she does not deny her gender."

I scan the pictures on the wall, searching for the familiar hieroglyphics that spell out Hatshepsut's pharaoh name, Maatkare, but I don't see them. Parts of the wall have been damaged, methodically scraped away so that instead of a figure in profile, there's the imprint of where one used to be, like the scarred ghost of the image. I lay the palm of my hand on the rough exposed rock, and a searing pain shoots through me as if I've touched a hot stove.

"Ow!" I grimace, pulling my hand away. For a second, I wonder if I'm being punished for breaking one of the cardinal rules of archeology—don't touch the art.

"You aren't supposed to do that!" Adom accuses me. "You know what Dad says."

Rashid shakes his head. "I say it, too—you should not touch these things!"

"I know!" My throbbing hand feels like it's been dipped in scalding water. "But there's no art there— that's what's so weird. Why did someone chisel off part of the scene? Was it a kind of censorship?"

Rashid shakes his head. "Not censorship, no, but an

erasure, an attempt to rewrite history. Do you see any cartouches with Maatkare's name on this wall?"

"No," I answer. "I was wondering about that." A dull ache spreads from my fingers up my wrist. I try not to think about the pain. If I ignore it, it will go away. At least that's what I tell myself.

"They have all been scraped away, sometimes re-carved with her father's name, Thutmose I, sometimes left as gashes in the stone. The same with some of the images of Hatshepsut, like the one you touched. Some have been left intact, others chiseled off. The worst damage was done on the highest terrace, where originally there were giant figures of Hatshepsut as the god Osiris. All of those statues were removed and thrown into a pit nearby."

I feel sick to my stomach. Dad's taught me enough so I know what that means—a kind of second death, a killing of the soul. "Why would anyone do that? Hatshepsut was a good pharaoh."

"There are several theories," Rashid begins.

Of course there are, I think, there always are, and we have to listen to all of them. I brace myself for a long lecture. I'm interested in Hatshepsut, but not in modern ideas about her that could be totally wrong. Theory is just another word for a guess. The only person I trust to tell me the truth about Hatshepsut is Meru. But I'm not going to say anything about Meru to Rashid, so I try to look fascinated as he continues.

"Historians used to think that Thutmose III removed any evidence of his stepmother in a vengeful rage because she took his throne from him. But the timing is not right. We now know that the damage was not done until the very end of Thutmose's reign, hardly the time for an angry outburst against his long-dead stepmother. So the destruction has to fit in with Thutmose's old age, and what makes the most sense is that by erasing Hatshepsut's existence, he could pretend that he was the direct, royal heir to Thutmose II, that he himself was of royal blood and so could legitimately pass on the crown to his own son. The erasure of Hatshepsut's names and images is not thorough or systematic. Only in the most public places, in the most recognized monuments, and it did not last long—another piece of evidence that suggests his own son's succession as pharaoh was the reason, since once his heir was accepted as the new king, the damage stopped."

The pain in my hand eases, but I'm left with a very clear impression of how horrible the scraping off of her name and image would have been for Hatshepsut.

"Since not all of her names were erased, does that mean Hatshepsut's soul didn't suffer from the destruction?" I ask. My hand feels almost normal now. If it could recover, could Hatshepsut?

Rashid narrows his eyes. "Are you talking about what the ancient Egyptians believed happened to her soul, or what I believe? Do I even believe we have souls? Do you?"

I smile back at him. You don't have a soul, that's for sure, I want to snap at him, but I don't. "I mean the ancient Egyptians, of course."

"Of course." Rashid's lips curve up in his usual attempt at a smile. "I think the ancient Egyptians would say that as long as the dead person's name exists somewhere, as long as there is a home for the soul in the tomb, no real harm has been done. It is safe to say that Thutmose III did not want to condemn his stepmother to a cruel soul death. He just wanted legitimacy for his son. He did the minimum to assure that and still preserve Hatshepsut's name and image, as well as her tomb." Rashid pauses. "Of course, if the soul was not happy with its place in the Field of Reeds, it could always choose to be reborn into a new body. Most souls would not chance another earthly life. Someone who lived as a pharaoh could be reborn a beggar. Why risk that?"

Or worse, I think, they could be reborn as *you*. But I feel better knowing that Hatshepsut wasn't doomed to a horrible soul death. I look again at the hand that touched the scarred stone. It's still red, even though it doesn't hurt anymore. If that searing pain was anything like what Hatshepsut felt when the chisel gashed away at her image, that would be torment enough.

Adom tugs at my shirt. "We've seen this part long enough. Can we go up to the highest level now? I want to see what's up there."

"Good idea," I say. I wish I could escape Rashid. Since I can't, I promise myself not to talk to him anymore. He can lecture all he wants, but I won't ask any more questions.

Rashid starts to lead us up the ramp when a woman in a big sun hat and brightly flowered shorts taps him on the shoulder.

"I couldn't help hearing what you said. It was fascinating, completely fascinating," she gushes in a Texas twang. "I wonder if you wouldn't mind answering some questions my husband and I have." She turns and points to a thick, balding man sweating next to her.

"Do you mind, children," she asks Adom and me, "if we borrow your knowledgeable father for a few minutes? We'll give him right back, I promise."

Ick! I think, he's *not* my father. But what I say is, "Of course, please take your time. You're lucky to have found such a good guide."

Rashid smiles graciously and waves us up the ramp. "Yes, madam?" he asks, clearly pleased to be recognized for the expert that he is.

Adom and I hurry to the third terrace. This is definitely a place I want to explore without Rashid. I remember Meru's description of the secret Senenmut showed him and I wonder if the shrine still stands, if the evidence of Senenmut's sacrilege was ever discovered. Maybe that's why he disappeared. It wasn't jealousy about another woman that threw him into exile, but the priests finding out about his sacrilege.

The ramp opens onto a broad colonnade like the terrace below, but along with reliefs on the walls, this level is decorated by imposing statues in front of some of the columns, facing the Nile. These are the sculptures Rashid mentioned, the ones of Hatshepsut as Osiris. Only a few have been restored, but originally each column would have had its own Osiris figure. Shadows of a few tourists appear and disappear behind the columns, but mostly we have the place to ourselves. There is an elderly couple posing for a souvenir photo, a small group of young backpackers, and us. No, there are two more people—Meru and Senenmut. They're here, too.

Mothers

THE VIEW FROM THE HIGH TERRACE IS impressive. Looking toward the mountains is not nearly so rewarding. The walls are crumbling fragments. A few remaining columns stab the deep blue sky like jagged teeth. I can't tell which pile of rubble was Hatshepsut's shrine and which was something else entirely. Pieces of sculpture and sections of wall carvings are heaped up, waiting for archeologists to catalog and restore them to their original positions. Senenmut's daring portraits are somewhere in the jumble, but I have no idea how to find them. Does it really matter, I wonder. Do I need to see them? Isn't it enough to know that he was close enough to Hatshepsut to dare such a thing?

I sketch the pile of broken columns and carvings, hoping my eye can sort out the mess, but I can't find any order in the wreckage, any sense of what Hatshepsut's holiest shrine would have looked like.

Why do I care so much about all of this? Because I do, I realize. I feel connected to the story in some weird way, like it's my own family history, not a dusty ancient mystery. But I've come to a dead end at the temple.

Adom has finished his running tour of the terrace and is back in front of me again. "Okay, I've seen everything. This part is in bad shape. Let's go back down. Maybe there's a gift shop or a snack place."

I shake my head. Naturally those are the things that most interest Adom. "You're hungry already? You should have eaten a bigger breakfast, like I told you to."

"You're not my mother, you know," Adom snaps. "You're my way-too-bossy sister."

I glare at my brother. He's happy enough for me to cuddle him and rock him to sleep, to kiss his scrapes and help him with his homework, to pack his lunches and cook his dinner, all those things Mom used to do before she died. I've been taking care of Adom for years now, even though Dad still pretends to do it. It's not like I asked for the job, either. It just sort of happened. Dad was so sad that first year, he disappeared in a way, staying in his darkened bedroom for hours. Adom would wail that he was hungry, but Dad wouldn't answer. So I started making things—at first simple stuff you could cook in a microwave, then real food like macaroni and cheese or enchiladas. Dad didn't notice the dirty laundry piling up, so I taught myself how to use the washing machine and dryer. He would have let Adom stay up all night, so I started reading to him and tucking him into bed. I admit Dad's better now, he's not so lost in his grief anymore, but I still do way more than most kids I know. That's why it's so annoying when Dad acts like he can't trust me with Adom. I take way better care of him than Dad does!

Adom knows it, too. He comes to me when he's scared or hurt or has a problem at school. But something's changed with him on this trip. He gets mad at me quickly and his feelings get hurt more easily. Maybe he's as confused by being in Egypt as I am. Or maybe—I hope not—he's turning into a teenager, even though he's only ten.

I know I should be patient with him either way, but I'm too annoyed to stay calm. I snap back.

"I never said I was your mother!" I turn and stride away. "You're such a brat, such a pest! I didn't ask you to follow me! I didn't say I'd take care of you!"

Adom is frozen, stunned, but I don't care. I don't look back, not even once, as I stomp down the ramp, past the second terrace, down to the first terrace, and out of the temple. Tears sting my eyes. If I passed Rashid, my vision was too blurred for me to notice. I walk until I see a passageway to the side of the temple, a place where I can hide in a dark corner and let loose all my tears. I'm not crying because Adom is ungrateful or a brat. I'm crying, great heaving sobs, because I want someone to take care of *me*. I want someone to be *my* mother. And somehow being here, in this place, makes the need feel bigger and rawer than ever. I thought I'd gotten over Mom's death. I hardly thought of her anymore. Until we came here and the sands shifted.

Starry Skies

I CRY UNTIL MY EYES FEEL GRAINY AND MY throat is raw. It's strange how much I seem to cry these days. I don't remember crying much at all when Mom died, and it's like all those pent-up tears are rushing out now that we're in the place where she was born, where she grew up.

When I'm calm again, I walk to the souvenir and snack stalls set up by the parking lot. I'm curious to see if there are small stone models of the temple like the one the old woman gave me, but all I see is the familiar mix of wooden cobras, leather camels, and piles of dusty post-cards. I look around for Adom but he's not there, either. Rashid is, though. He sees me and grabs me by the arm.

"There you are! You are always getting lost! I wish

you would stay with me instead of wandering off on your own. And where is your brother? I thought he was with you!" Rashid tightens his grip.

"No," I say. "And can you please let go?" I shake my arm free. "I'm not running away or anything. Neither is Adom—he's still on the upper terrace."

"I looked there. I looked everywhere for both of you. Now I find you, but not him. Where could he be?" Rashid's voice vibrates with suppressed panic. Hearing it, I can't help but feel anxious, too, even though I'm sure Adom is someplace obvious, like the bathroom or waiting for us by the jeep.

"Don't worry," I say. "He's got to be somewhere. You check the men's room. I'll look around the car."

We agree to meet back by the jeep. The parking lot is still nearly empty—a few cars, a tour bus, and some peddlers hawking postcards and cheap bracelets away from the competition of the stands. There's no sign of Adom. Rashid's driver is leaning on the jeep, smoking. He smiles at me and throws down the cigarette.

"Are you ready to go now?" he asks in careful English.

"Soon," I say, "but we need to find my brother first. Have you seen him?"

The driver shakes his head.

When I see Rashid striding toward us without Adom, I begin to worry, too. Where could he be?

"Wait here," I tell Rashid. "Let me look on the upper terrace again."

"It is no use, I just searched there," Rashid protests.

"I want to look, too," I insist.

Rashid shakes his head and turns to the driver, speaking rapid-fire Arabic. Whatever he says sounds more ominous because I can't understand it.

Back on the highest terrace, I poke through the piles of rubble, thinking maybe Adom crawled into some dark corner to hide, but I don't see anything except carved stone faces. My stomach is churning with fear now. What could have happened to Adom?

A movement in the far corner catches my eye. It's a bird, I tell myself, or a snake, something small, not boy-sized. I come closer. I don't see any birds or lizards, but I do see a profile that's familiar somehow. I bend down and trace my finger along the brow and nose. I feel the strange magnetic pull again, like I can't take my hand away, and I feel certain that it's Senenmut, carved on a fragment that's jutting out of the rubble. My finger follows the contours of his chin, ending abruptly where the carving has broken off, and with it breaks the strange connection I felt with the face. I place my hand back on the face, and suddenly I'm standing in a small shrine. In the flicker of torchlight, the figure of Senenmut and its twin flank the closed wooden doors. The portraits seem to move, dancing and praying. They're the same images that Senenmut showed Meru, the ones that placed him next to his lover through all of eternity. Or so the architect thought. He didn't know that thousands of years later, the shrine would be a jumble of pieces, his place with Hatshepsut taken away from him. He didn't know that she would be searching for him, asking some stranger to find him.

"Here he is," I whisper and reach out to touch one of the carvings, whole now. It wavers and disappears in a swirl of mist and I'm back in the sunshine again, among the ruined stones. I look again at the slab with Senenmut's portrait, now a sad, broken piece of rubble. I sketch it, but the connection is gone. It's just a piece of stone.

For a minute, I found Senenmut. He was there, before me. Now I'm alone again and Adom is missing. I rub my eyes, trying to clear my vision. I feel the way I do after an especially vivid dream, as if I'm in some in-between place where both the dream and the real world have the same weight, the same hold over me. The things I imagined seem as real as what's around me now. I was in Hatshepsut's shrine, I know it. I saw the carvings, just as Meru described them.

"Talibah!" Rashid calls me from the steps leading to the terrace. "Did you find him?"

I'm firmly back in the here and now, back to worrying about Adom. "No," I yell down. "But he must be somewhere. He can't have just vanished." But even as I say the words, I wonder if that's exactly what happened—if he disappeared in the mist along with the carving of Senenmut, if he's trapped in some spirit world of ancient Egyptian magic. I'm more than worried now. I'm terrified.

We search every inch of the temple. Nothing. It's been an hour since we first started looking, and it seems a bad sign that so much time has passed with no hint of Adom. We ask everyone we run into, but no one has seen a slender boy in a bright red T-shirt with black hair and enormous brown eyes.

I scour the expanse between the temple and the parking lot, the place where there was a green garden many, many years ago, with fountains and exotic trees and birds. Now there is sand and stone and bits of sculpture, along with the occasional plastic bag and scrap of paper. I find a hollow in the ground, hidden by a slight rise. Coming closer, I see it's a hole. Could it be an old well? Maybe Adom fell in! I call to Rashid and show him what I've found.

"Look," I say, "it's like a tunnel into the ground." I can see now that there's a ladder against the side of the hole. Adom could have easily climbed down it.

Rashid nods. "Yes, it is an entrance to a tomb. It must be Senenmut's. I know it is somewhere around here, though I have never bothered to explore it before. No one has sealed it off because there is nothing inside to steal. But really, it presents a hazard for foolish tourists. I will advise the authorities about it." There's an edge of distaste to Rashid's voice and I wonder if he's afraid to go underground—a strange phobia for someone who's excavating a tomb.

"Like any good archeologist, I always have a flashlight with me." Rashid pulls a slender flashlight out of his pocket and turns on the bright beam. "I hope

Adom is here. And that he did not meet a scorpion on his way."

I follow Rashid down the ladder. It doesn't take long to reach the bottom, and soon we're in a corridor that slopes gently downward. There's no decoration on the walls, so I would never have suspected it was a tomb. The descent continues for a long time, pitching more steeply and curving around until it opens up into a small chamber. There in the middle of the room, with his own flashlight trained on the ceiling, is Adom.

"Adom!" I run to grab him, to press him to me. I'm so relieved that he's okay, that he's here in this world, not magicked away by some mummy's curse. Then I'm mad, furious even. "What were you thinking?" I push him away, holding him firmly by the shoulders. "You know you're not supposed to wander off on your own!"

"You said you didn't want me following you! You said you didn't want to take care of me anymore!" Adom's eyes are red, and I can see he's been crying.

I hug him again, gently this time. "I'm sorry. I lost my temper. You really had me worried. I promise I'll try not to yell at you anymore, and you need to promise not to run away."

Adom nods, snuffling into my armpit.

Rashid pulls Adom roughly by the neck of his shirt. "This was bad of you!" he shouts. "Very bad! You cannot wander around as you please!"

Adom looks stunned and I fold my arms around him. "You don't need to scream like that," I say.

"I do, I do need to scream!" Rashid eyes bulge in anger. "The temple is a sacred place, a holy place. You should walk around it with respect. And you should not wander into bad places. This is an evil place! I should not be here!"

"Evil?" I ask. "I thought you said this was Senenmut's tomb. Why would that be a bad place?"

"It's not a bad place!" Adom is defiant. "Senenmut? I know I've heard that name before—I wish I could remember where. And this a really cool place. See what I found!"

Rashid takes deep breaths, trying to calm himself. He really is a nutcase, I decide. Either he's Dr. Jekyll, lecturing at you, or he's Mr. Hyde, a crocodile-toothed monster.

"What?" I ask Adom. "What did you discover?"

"This," Adom says, directing his flashlight at the ceiling again. "Look, it's really cool—it's a map of the stars at night, like ancient Egyptian constellations."

Adom's right—the ceiling is amazing. I try to capture its complexity in my sketchbook, but the flashlight beam isn't steady and I can't draw the whole thing.

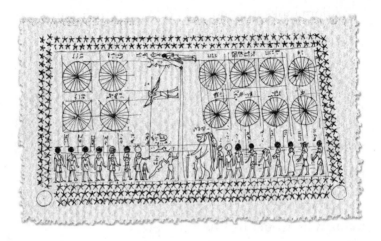

"Yes, that is exactly what it is," Rashid croaks, joining his beam to Adom's, giving me more light for sketching. The breathing technique must have worked because the rage has been shoved down and he's back to being Dr. Jekyll. "This is the first representation of the night sky known to exist. It is almost thirty-five hundred years old."

"And is this Senenmut's tomb?" I repeat, shivering, suddenly realizing where I am. This is where the architect's *ka*—or soul—would live if all the tomb furnishings were still here.

"Yes," Rashid answers, his voice still hoarse with

anger. "Senenmut had an unusual, original mind, as you can see from the temple he built for Hatshepsut, and for his own tomb he chose to paint the night sky as it had never been depicted before, with an astronomic representation of the constellations."

"What happened to his mummy?" I ask. "Where's all the stuff they found in here when the tomb was discovered?"

Rashid is still looking up at the ceiling, but his tone is sharp. Mr. Hyde is creeping back in. "There was no mummy, no 'stuff,' as you so eloquently put it. All they found was a cracked stone sarcophagus—empty. And this sarcophagus, meant for Senenmut's mummy, was made of the same stone reserved for royal burials. There is no other private sarcophagus like it—none! What right did he have to a royal burial like that, directly underneath the pharaoh's mortuary temple—in a royal sarcophagus? Such impudence! His mummy has never turned up. And I think it never will. It seems from the way his name has been erased from monuments that the architect fell into sudden disfavor. There is no mention of him in the ancient records after a certain date—an abrupt and complete silence. A silence I am sure he deserved. Now we must go—as I said, this is an evil place."

I shiver again, filled with an icy chill. So Senenmut did disappear. Or was wiped out of official memory. This place should feel full of his energy, his spirit, but it's cold and empty. The only impression I have is one of desolation, of absence. I felt closer to Senenmut in the temple, especially on the topmost terrace. Here, there is nothing but the cold painted stars on the ceiling.

Soul Deaths

BACK AT THE HOTEL, THERE'S A MESSAGE from Dad. Instead of coming tomorrow like he'd planned, he says he'll be a couple of days late. Rashid looks irritated to be saddled with us for even longer. I tell him we're fine on our own, but he just scowls and says he'll meet us after breakfast. He's finally taking us to his famous tomb.

It's been an exhausting day. I want to soak in a hot bath but Adom is still buzzing. He isn't mad at me anymore and is so excited by everything we've seen, by the promise of seeing more, he's having a hard time winding down. After the mortuary temple of Hatshepsut, I wanted to come back, to collapse at the hotel. But Rashid insisted we go to the Valley of the Queens, where we went into several more tombs. It was as if he had to erase the sensation of Senenmut's tomb by immersing himself in different ones. At first I thought Adom and I would feel dragged along on a grown-up errand, like when Dad tells us we're stopping at the hardware store on the way home and it'll only take a moment, but then an hour later we're still wandering through aisles of plumbing supplies and pipe wrenches. Luckily, it wasn't like that at all. Rashid may have needed the contrast of these richly painted tombs to the emptiness of Senenmut's. To Adom and me, they were simply beautiful. The colors of the carvings were as fresh as the day they were painted—rich, buttery yellows, vibrant reds, soft, powdery blues. The scenes of bread baking, men fishing, and women dancing were full of life and movement. I was surprised that they could be thousands of years old and still look so bright. It was as if someone like Meru had worked there only yesterday. Copying the scenes in my sketchbook, I had the warm sensation that I was walking in his world. That helped take away the chill that Senenmut's tomb had soaked into my bones.

After I finally settle Adom in bed, I open the silver book. I thought I was too tired to read, but I'm too full of images from the tombs, from the temple not to. I want to hear Meru's voice again, to walk alongside him and see what happens next.

Two days before her wedding, Princess Neferure died. A strange illness came and took her quickly. No doctor or scorpion charmer could help. She went to bed with a high fever and never awoke. So instead of celebratory songs, now we hear funeral chants, the cries and wailing of mourners, and the heavy, thick, suffocating silence of black sorrow.

Neferure died? I mean, of course I know she's dead because she lived thousands of years ago, but I assumed she married Thutmose, had kids, and lived until the ripe old age of forty or however long people lived then. I don't know anything about her except her name, but tears are running down my face. I'm crying for some long-ago dead person I never knew, which makes no sense at all. But I can't help myself. I cry as if my best friend had died, as if someone very close to me was gone.

Even though Adom's a sound sleeper, I try to stifle my sobs. I don't want to wake him—I don't want to worry him again. I take deep breaths, and when my eyes aren't blurred by tears anymore, I pick up the book again.

Senenmut is a hollow, broken man. His gray skin sags, all the old charm is sucked out of him, leaving him a dry husk. Hapuseneb, on the other hand, crackles with energy, an angry, determined willfulness. He is sure that Senenmut is responsible for Neferure's death, that he poisoned her somehow, and the high priest is eagerly spreading this rumor to all who will listen.

I warn Senenmut of Hapuseneb's evil words and suggest that he should leave the city of Thebes for a while, anything to keep him away from vicious tongues and plots. But my uncle refuses.

"I must be here to protect myself, to prove my loyalty to Hatshepsut. She knows how I loved Neferure. She knows the truth of my heart. I will not be chased away by that snake of a high priest. Hapuseneb has always been my enemy. Now Thutmose is as well. Because of who I am, of my closeness to the Pharaoh. I must stand by her side now more than ever. This is not the time to be a coward."

I wonder if Neferure's death could have been another reason for Senenmut's disappearance. If Hapuseneb succeeded in making everyone think that Senenmut poisoned the princess, the architect would have been killed or exiled, and he certainly wouldn't have been mummified. A royal murderer wouldn't get that kind of honor. I feel sure Senenmut wasn't guilty, but I wonder if that's what happened. So now there are four possible reasons for his vanishing. One, he cheated on Hatshepsut (with Neferure or someone else). Two, the priests found out about the sacrilegious portraits of Senenmut in the pharaoh's shrine. Three, he killed Neferure to prevent her from marrying Thutmose, or even if he didn't kill her, the pharaoh believed he did. Four, maybe there's another entirely different reason that I haven't figured out yet!

And I wonder about Neferure. Where is her mummy? Is her *ka* taken care of in the afterlife? Or is her spirit unsettled because it was snatched from this world too soon? Maybe she took the risk of being reborn because her earthly life was so short. Or maybe she's haunting this place and that's why there was the voice asking for her.

I don't want the fate of an ancient princess who died young to be intertwined with mine. I don't want Hatshepsut to call on me to find Senenmut because she thinks I'm some kind of stand-in for her long-dead daughter, even if we do look alike. And I definitely don't want to be taken over by someone else's soul, even a royal princess's. If I'm to do this, to find Senenmut for the pharaoh, it has to be because of who I am, not who I'm substituting for. That's why Hatshepsut should choose me—because she wants a strong, smart girl for the job, someone like herself. Neferure seems sweet, but wimpy. After all, she's willing to marry Thutmose III because she's supposed to. She does what she's told. I'm not like that. I'd rather be like Queen Elizabeth I than some coddled princess.

It strikes me that maybe Hatshepsut isn't asking Neferure to conduct this search. After all, she knew her daughter died and where she was entombed. Something even worse must have happened to Senenmut or the pharaoh wouldn't be looking for him. To an ancient Egyptian, there's only one thing worse than death—that's soul death, the kind of erasure that Rashid described in Senenmut's tomb. I remember the lonely emptiness in the tomb. There wasn't the violent anguish I would expect if Senenmut had been buried there and the tomb later robbed and desecrated. It was blank, as if he'd never been buried, as if his soul had never had a mummy to enter into. No body to preserve for the afterlife? That would definitely be a fate much worse than any death.

I try to read more, but the words blur together. I can't keep my eyes from closing. I slip the book under my pillow and fall into a deep sleep. When I wake up in the morning, I can't remember any dreams, only blankness and more blankness.

14

Another Gift

WHEN I COME OUT OF THE SHOWER, Adom is waiting right in front of the door, hopping from one foot to the other.

"Look, Talibah," he says, thrusting a small package at me. "This came for you while you were in the bathroom. Open it! Let's see what it is!"

"How strange," I say, taking the paper-wrapped box. "Who is it from?" There's nothing written on it, except my name in careful square letters. I wonder if there's a note inside. I tear open the dark brown paper to reveal a cardboard box. I lift the lid and peer inside. There's no note, only a small stone sculpture nestled in shredded newspaper. Like the model of Hatshepsut's temple, the carving is detailed and shows a man seated so that his lap and legs are morphed into an abstract box, making his pose solid and forceful. I recognize Senenmut's characteristic profile. It's a small figurine of the man I'm looking for. The most unusual part of the sculpture is the tiny child's head that juts out of the box, like a diagrammatic model of a child in someone's lap. The child is literally contained by the man, held safe and secure by him. It's hard to explain in words, but a drawing shows it:

"Wow!" Adom says. "It's beautiful! How come you keep getting these cool statues? Who gave this to you?"

He runs a finger over Senenmut's jet-black profile. "You can't even buy stuff like this in the souvenir stalls. This is really special." Adom studies me carefully. "What's going on? Do you have some rich Egyptian boyfriend?"

"What?" I say. "I don't know who this is from. There's no note or anything. Who brought it to the door?"

"Someone from the hotel," Adom answers. "I didn't ask who gave it to them to deliver. And what is it, anyway? Why is this little head sticking out?"

I turn the sculpture around in my hand, studying it from every angle, but there's no answer written on it except in hieroglyphs I don't understand. I don't know what it means, what it represents, except that the man is definitely Senenmut.

"Wait a minute," I say. "Did you notice anything unusual about the person who brought this?"

"What do you mean 'unusual'? It was just an ordinary guy," Adom insists.

"He was wearing a bracelet, right, a golden snake with ruby eyes?" I'm sure of the answer even before I ask the question.

Adom squints in thought. "Yeeaaaaah, I think he was. Does that mean something?"

"Come on," I tell Adom. "Let's get dressed and have

breakfast. We can figure this out later." But I feel like I've discovered an important part of the mystery. The Servants of Hatshepsut must still exist! They're working for their beloved pharaoh, helping to lead me the right way so I can discover what happened to Senenmut. The odd sculpture must be a clue, something to point me toward the truth. But why me?

Adom shrugs. "Okay. Let's ask Rashid. I bet he knows what it is and who it's from."

"I don't want Rashid to know anything about it!" My tone is sharp, though I try to soften it.

Adom looks at me more suspiciously than ever. "Okaaaaaay," he drawls, measuring me with his eyes. "I won't tell Rashid about this particular sculpture, but I'll tell him I saw one like it at a souvenir stand and ask him what it is."

"Fine," I say. "You can do that so long as you don't say a word—not one word—about either of the carvings I have. They're none of his business."

"Grouchy, grouchy . . . ," Adom mutters. "Must be too early in the day for Talibah to be human yet."

My backpack now holds quite a collection—the silver book, the model of Hatshepsut's temple, and the seated figure of Senenmut. They're too valuable to leave in the hotel room. I need to have them with me, to keep them safe. They all seem like important parts of the same puzzle. They all tell me something about Senenmut. Too bad I'm not sure what.

After breakfast, we meet Rashid to cross the Nile again, this time to go to the tomb he's excavating. As we bump along in the jeep driving toward the Valley of the Nobles, Adom asks him about the strange little statue.

Rashid rubs his forehead, puzzled. "Of course I know those kinds of statues, but I have never seen models of them. They are not the usual tourist-type subject."

"I guess the seller at this stall wanted something different to offer tourists other than the same old, same old," Adom explains. "Anyway, what is it? Who is it?"

Rashid is clearly unsettled by the idea of such an odd souvenir, but he can't help giving a textbook answer. "The man is Senenmut, the architect who built the temple we saw yesterday. He was also the tutor of Hatshepsut's daughter and held a privileged position because of his close relationship with the princess. He had numerous statues made of him with his young charge, inventing a subject for monumental sculpture that had not existed before, the tutor with his royal pupil. There are many of these statues, most with Senenmut seated like you described, others with him standing and cradling his young student. They can be quite tender and sweet, more like a father and a daughter than anything else, but I have always considered them to be flaunting his closeness to the royal family. A position he, with his common blood, did not deserve at all."

Of course Rashid can't resist taking a jab at Senenmut. He furrows his brows as if he's about to really go off, then changes his mind and falls back into his lecturing tone.

"The one you describe is more formal and stylized, with the block for the body and legs containing all but the head of the girl. This was the subject that Senenmut chose to mark his own tomb—not a statue of himself as architect or administrator for the pharaoh, but of himself holding Neferure. I told you he could not resist boasting."

"But we were at his tomb and I didn't see any sculpture," I say, ignoring the snide insult.

"That was his second tomb, the one he meant to be buried in, so he could be close to Hatshepsut—an outrageous idea! The first tomb is in the Valley of the Nobles and was started before Senenmut attained so much power. It is where Senenmut should have been buried, not anywhere near the pharaoh's temple. The tomb is marked at the entrance by a large statue just like the one you describe."

I touch my backpack gently. So I have images of both Senenmut and Neferure in a sculpture that links the two of them as closely as possible. It's almost like Senenmut is pregnant with the princess, encompassing her in his own body. I like that idea, and I can't help but imagine what it must have felt like for Neferure to be so treasured, so nurtured, so protected. I want to feel that safe. I want to feel that loved.

Of course I know that Dad loves me. Sometimes he's too protective, but since Mom died, he has only half a heart. At least, that's how it seems to me. There's a scooped-out, hollow part inside of him, an emptiness I can't touch—and I don't want to touch it anyway. I remember that I used to wish Dad was the one who had died instead of Mom. She wouldn't have collapsed into her sadness and left us to fend for ourselves the way he did. Then I felt guilty for wishing that. It wasn't Dad's fault. He was doing the best he could. But it wasn't enough. It was never enough.

I look over at Adom. I wonder if he's thinking the same thing, if he's jealous of Neferure, of the love and care she got from Senenmut. I put my arm around him and pull him closer. "Thanks for asking," I whisper into his ear. "I'm glad we found out about the statue, and I sure didn't want to bring it up."

Adom nods and winks at me. I feel an intense rush of love for him. He's so sweet and loyal, so little and vulnerable. It's strange, but feeling protective of him makes me feel much stronger myself. I don't need someone to take care of me—I just need to be sure I take good care of Adom.

The jeep stops in front of a boarded-up opening in the low hills.

Rashid jumps out and starts unlocking the heavy padlock that secures a chain wrapped around the two boards gaping across the makeshift entrance. It doesn't look official at all—just plywood connected to posts, with a gap between them because the boards don't even quite meet each other. A stray cat could easily squeeze between them, even shut, since only the padlocked chain holds them closed. I'm surprised a tomb robber hasn't broken in already.

"Here we are!" Rashid says, pulling open one board. "Now it is obvious that there is a tomb here, but believe me, when I came to this place, it looked like the rest of the landscape—there was nothing to mark the site of a tomb. I just felt it in my gut. I knew it, knew it more forcefully than I have ever known anything, as soon as I stepped in front of this place. It was uncanny!" Rashid sounds younger, almost boyish in his excitement. For a second, I almost like him.

He turns on the powerful flashlight he brought with him, much bigger than the tiny Maglite he had yesterday, and gestures for us to follow him. As we follow the corridor, he describes the moment of discovery, how perfectly preserved the interior was, what an important contribution he's making to the study of ancient Egypt. He doesn't pause for breath, but keeps on talking, the words blurring together in my head in a steady stream of self-congratulation.

As we go farther in, a sharp wave of nausea hits me. It's so strong, I have to stop. My forehead is clammy with sweat and I double over in pain. Adom is ahead of me and doesn't notice anything's wrong. I try to breathe slowly, pushing down the urge to turn around and run. I force my feet forward, continuing down the sloping corridor deep into the earth. The images on the walls on either side of me dance and grimace, mocking me. From a muffled distance, I hear shrill demonic laughter, as if I'm getting closer to hell. I shake my head, trying to clear my eyes and ears. The evil laughter fades away and the paintings on the wall freeze into place, but something feels very wrong.

I meet up with Adom and Rashid in the central burial chamber. Hapuseneb's mummy still sits in its heavy stone sarcophagus, surrounded by statues, pottery, jewelry, chairs, a jumble of supplies for the afterlife. Rashid points out where the photographers have set up their equipment.

"Everything will be recorded before being moved to the Cairo museum," he explains. "You have arrived at a unique moment—after the clearing away of rubble and dirt, but before the cataloging and packing away of all the material has begun. It's a rare chance to see a tomb much as it was when it was sealed almost three and a half millennia ago."

Adom is so excited, he doesn't know what to ask. I wait for the barrage of "what's this?" and "who's that?" but there's a stunned silence. Adom's eyes are enormous with wonder and he walks slowly around the chamber, savoring every detail, examining each treasure with awe. Rashid watches him, smiling with pride. He's bursting with the urge to explain everything from the leather sandals to the scarab amulets. Adom doesn't need to ask a thing. Rashid will tell us anyway. Nothing could stop him. He starts by talking about the sarcophagus, the hieroglyphics on it, how he discovered it was Hapuseneb's tomb that he had stumbled onto. Rashid points out the cartouche with Hapuseneb's name, the clue he needed to identify the tomb's owner. I stare at the name cartouche lit by the glare of Rashid's flashlight. I know I've seen it somewhere else, but I can't think of where. It's a complicated image and I sketch it quickly, so I can figure out later where I recognize it from.

Adom listens and I try to pay attention, too, but I'm distracted by the paintings on the walls. Like the ones in the corridor earlier, the figures start to pulse and move. I feel a stab of recognition—they're the images from my dream that first night in Egypt. They shift and transform from one elusive thing into another until one section comes into crystal-clear focus. I see Hapuseneb standing by the Nile, a crocodile on the shore across from him. The next scene shows the dead man's heart being weighed, just like the picture in the Book of the Dead. I watch in horror as the heart sinks. It's much heavier than the feather, black with the weight of its evil deeds. There is a piercing shriek and the hungry demon leaps at Hapuseneb, swallowing him in one awful gulp. The painting melts on the wall, dripping down to the floor like blood. I gasp, my mouth dry and chalky, my eyes riveted by the swirl of red at my feet. When I dare to look up at the wall again, the painting is back to its original form, the heart being weighed, the demon waiting, Hapuseneb standing by, secure in the purity of his soul.

I look at Adom. Did he notice anything? Had I imagined the whole thing? My brother is still transfixed by the mummy. If there was a shriek, he didn't hear it. Rashid, however, is pale and sweating. Did he see the same vision?

Rashid wipes his forehead with a handkerchief. He turns the heavy ring on his finger nervously. Suddenly he's not as eager to lecture. Adom senses the change in our guide.

"Is something the matter?" he asks.

"No, no, nothing," Rashid hastily reassures us. "Only I do not want anything touched or moved. You are very lucky to have seen this much, but we really should not stay any longer."

"I didn't touch anything!" Adom thinks he's being punished for something he hasn't done, that Rashid is unfairly suspicious.

"I did not say you had." There's a greenish tinge to Rashid's skin and I wonder if he's feeling as nauseated as I am, if he wants to get out of this suffocating cave as much as I do.

"But you think I will!" Adom persists.

"No!" Rashid croaks. "It is time to go, that is all. No reasons necessary. You had the privilege to see this—that is enough! You should be thanking me, not talking back to me!"

There's no response to this. Adom's had his treasured moment, but it's tainted by Rashid's nastiness. And this isn't something I'm imagining. This isn't a vague intuition. It's definite proof that Rashid's a total creep.

I touch Adom lightly on the shoulder. "You were right about this being very cool," I tell him. "But let's go now. I bet we'll have another chance to come here when Dad meets us."

"That is right!" Rashid tries to sound jolly. "We will come back with your father, I promise." He turns to lead us out, the bright light raking the walls, casting eerie shadows of jackal heads and rearing cobras.

I follow Adom, relieved we're finally going, but just as I'm about to step out of the chamber and back into the corridor, I feel a strange tug. It's as if someone is pulling me by the elbow back into the room. I can't help it—I turn around, fumbling for the small flashlight on my key chain. I'm drawn to the great sarcophagus, pulled to the blackness of it. On the floor by the side of the heavy stone, something glitters in the dim light. Without thinking, I stoop down and pick up a ring. I feel a jolt as my fingers touch the icy metal. I know this is wrong, this is stealing, but I can't put the ring down, not back in this awful chamber. Instead, I tuck it carefully in my pocket. Instantly, I feel an enormous release, a lifting of the pressure that pulled me back into the room, and I hurry to follow the others out.

15

The Ring

RASHID SAYS HE CAN'T TAKE US TO THE VALLEY of the Kings as he had planned. Something has come up that he needs to do. At least that's the transparently fake excuse he gives. I think he wants to drop us off at the hotel because he's feeling sick. He's still pale and sweaty, with greenish circles under his eyes. Something happened to him in the tomb, something strange that he won't talk about.

Adom is disappointed but knows better than to complain. He doesn't want to be called ungrateful again. I'm relieved to have the time away from our guide so I can examine the ring. There has to be a reason I felt compelled to pick it up. In the dark gloom of the tomb it was a small glittering object, nothing more. I need light and time and privacy to see what it really is.

Back in our room after a quick lunch in the hotel dining room, I take out the ring and feel a jolt again as I touch it. I know it's simply an object, but it seems to vibrate with life in my hand. I remember when I was little, and Mom gave me a Mexican jumping bean. It was a plain brown bean, but she told me to keep it warm in the palm of my hand and something magical would happen. I stood there with my hand out, hardly daring to breathe, until the bean began to twitch.

"How does it do that?" I asked, both enthralled and scared by the mystery of it. I don't remember Mom's scientific, commonsense explanation, only the wonder of the bean jumping in my palm. That's what it feels like now with the ring in my hand. It's alive the way the bean was, only I'm sure there's no logical reason behind its energy.

The ring is a thick gold band striped with deep blue lapis lazuli framing a cartouche with a name inscribed in hieroglyphics. It looks like the kind of ring that's both jewelry and official seal, a symbol of status and power, a little like the ring Rashid wears, but this one is the opposite of creepy—it's powerful in a good way.

I don't recognize the name in the oblong frame. It's not Hatshepsut or her pharaoh name, Maatkare. And it's not Hapuseneb's. I hold it in one hand, sketching it with the other, admiring its elegance and beauty. I'm sure it belonged to someone important—it's fine enough to be a pharaoh's.

Adom looks over my shoulder. "What have you got now? Wow! That's even better than the sculptures!" He narrows his eyes, searching my face for some secret he's sure I'm hiding. "What's going on? Where did you get all these things? Are you stealing?"

"Of course not!" I protest, though that's exactly how I got the ring—and Meru's book—though I prefer to call it borrowing.

"Then where did you get them?"

"They're gifts, but it's hard to explain. I don't know who's giving them to me or why. It's kind of a mystery, and I'm trying to figure it out."

"A mystery?" Adom's eyes light up. He loves puzzles, tricks, riddles, and most of all, mysteries. I'll have to explain everything to him now or he'll never leave me alone.

I bite my lip. Should I really tell him what's been going on? I don't like lying, especially to him. And I'm tired of carrying such a heavy secret all by myself. I study his face, his eyes bright and eager, his head cocked like an attentive puppy with perked-up ears. I know he wants to ask a million questions but he doesn't want to be a pest, so he waits quietly. I think of how disappointed he must be that Rashid made us leave the tomb so quickly. I want to offer him something so he'll feel better, and all I have to give him is my confused mess of a mystery. I'm not sure how or what to tell him.

It's a calm silence, and somehow that helps. Once I start talking, it's easy for me to let the words spill out. As best I can, I tell Adom about the old woman, the dream, the visions, the snake bracelets, the way everything leads to Senenmut, Hatshepsut, and Neferure, but most of all to Senenmut, the man I'm supposed to find. I even show him the book I found, the translation of Meru's papyrus. Adom doesn't interrupt to ask any questions. He just listens carefully.

When I'm done explaining, though it's not much of an explanation—more like a series of strangely interconnected events—he still doesn't say anything, and I can tell he's trying to figure out what it all means. I don't expect him to come up with an answer, but just telling him what's been happening is an enormous relief. I didn't realize how hard it was to keep these secrets until I finally shared them. I look at Adom's slender fingers pulling at the tufts on the bedspread, and I'm glad he's the one I told.

"I know why Hatshepsut chose you," he says. "I know why this is your mystery to solve."

"What? How can you know that?" Of all the things I expected Adom to say, this certainly isn't one of them.

"Because now I remember where I heard the name Senenmut before. It's been bugging me the whole trip, driving me crazy trying to figure it out. Remember when we were in his tomb, I said I'd heard of Senenmut, I just couldn't remember what or who had told me. Now I remember—it was Mom."

My stomach flips just hearing Adom talk about Mom. It's something we never do, so I don't know what memories he has of her, though I doubt there are very many.

"What do you mean?" I ask. "How can you remember hearing a weird name like Senenmut when you were so little? Why would Mom talk to you about him anyway?"

Adom shakes his head. "I do remember. It's one of the few memories I have of Mom. I remember her telling me that there was something important she needed to talk to me about and that she knew I was too young to understand what she meant, but I'd be able to figure it out later. She was going to tell you, too, she said, but I guess she got too sick and forgot."

"What did she say?" I wonder why, if it was so important, she told Adom first and not me. I was nine already, able to remember things and write them down to look at later. And here I am, all these years later, charged with finding Senenmut—me, not my brother. It's not Adom's fault, but I'm hurt that Mom chose him for this and not me. But then I get a sinking feeling—what if she did tell me and I'm the one who forgot? I wish I could remember everything she said to me that last year before she died, but it's all a big blank to me, an erased year.

"I'm glad she told you," I assure Adom. "Go on, what did she say?"

"I can't remember exactly," he says. "Something about Senenmut being connected to our family, to us. I didn't know she was talking about someone who'd been dead for thousands of years. I thought he was a relative living in Egypt."

"Well, you're wrong about that part, obviously," I say. "So maybe you're wrong about the rest of it, too. You don't know if you even remember the right name."

"I'm not wrong," Adom pouts. "Okay, maybe Senenmut isn't our long-lost cousin, but you *are* looking for him. Maybe the reason isn't just so Hatshepsut can know where Senenmut is or what happened to him, but so that you'll find something Mom wanted us to have."

This is getting more and more far-fetched. I'm looking for Senenmut for the pharaoh *and* for my mother? "How come I don't hear Mom's voice in my dreams?" I point out. "It's always Hatshepsut's."

Adom shrugs. "You think it's Hatshepsut's. But maybe it's Mom's. Do you even remember what she sounded like? I don't."

"Of course I do!" I say. But my stomach tightens

because really I don't. I haven't been able to conjure up her voice in years.

I can tell Adom doesn't believe me because he changes the subject. "Let me see that ring again."

I hand him the heavy ring. I don't want to argue, but I can't shake off the sadness that Mom didn't trust me with her secret. Or if she did, I let her down by forgetting it. I'm not sure which is worse. I want to believe she told me and that she thought by telling Adom, too, she was being extra careful, hoping we'd each remember at least parts of the message, but it didn't work that way. I forgot anything to do with Senenmut and all Adom remembers is the name.

"I know whose ring this is!" Holding the ring up high, Adom bounces up and down on the bed in excitement. "I know, I know, I know! I figured it out!"

"Stop that!" I say. "You're going to lose the ring. Whose is it and how do you know?"

Adom flops down on the bed, panting, and hands me the ring. "Here, you keep it safe. I recognize the name in hieroglyphics. I'm surprised you didn't," he gloats.

"How could I recognize it? I haven't seen it before."

"Yes, you have!" Adom grins infuriatingly.

"Tell me! I'm in no mood for games," I growl.

"Look at the little sculpture you got yesterday, the one of Senenmut and Neferure."

This better not be a lame trick, I think as I reach into my backpack and take out the carefully wrapped statue. At first I don't know what Adom means, but then I see it, the cartouche on the front of the block representing Senenmut's lap and legs. A tingling runs through me. It's Senenmut's—the ring is Senenmut's! The hieroglyphics spell his name, and the ring would have been used as a seal for all his official documents. I draw both cartouches, side by side. They match exactly.

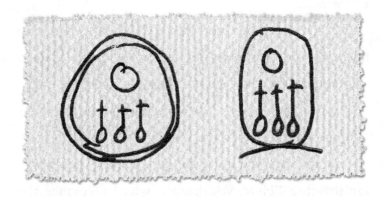

"I get it—you're right. This was Senenmut's ring!" I look at Adom, impressed that he remembered the cartouche on the statuette. If only he remembered exactly what Mom told him!

Adom nods happily. "And that's not the only place I've seen that hieroglyph. Look in the book you showed me—there was a small loose scrap of paper with a name cartouche. It's the same one!"

The paper that the old woman tucked into the book that day at the pool? I leaf through the pages and find it. Adom's right again. There's Senenmut's name printed in black ink.

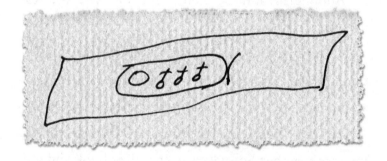

"Adom, you're amazing!" I say. "Everything points to Senenmut!"

"But how did the ring get in the high priest's tomb?" Adom asks, still bouncing on the bed in his excitement. "Why would Hapuseneb have Senenmut's ring?"

That's a good question. The answer to that might solve the mystery of what happened to Senenmut.

"Does Meru mention the ring?" Adom continues. "Maybe his book explains how Hapuseneb got it."

"I don't know," I admit. "I haven't finished reading it. He hasn't said anything so far about a ring."

"You haven't read the whole thing yet?" Adom is exasperated. "If I'd found something so cool, I'd have read it all in one gulp! What are you waiting for?"

"I haven't had time!" I feel vaguely guilty, like I've let Meru down, disappointed him by not being glued to his story until the end.

Adom grins at me. "There's time now. Will you read it to me?"

I start to protest that he's too old for that kind of thing. Then I realize it's not a bedtime story Adom is asking for. He wants to find out whatever Meru says at the same time I do. He wants us to figure out this mystery together. So I take out the silver book and start to read to my brother, something I haven't done in a very long time.

I went to work as usual the following morning and the day after that and the day after that. I did not see my uncle as I often did in passing, but I was absorbed with my own thoughts, so I did not notice his absence until the Pharaoh herself sent for me.

I had never seen Hatshepsut close up before. She had never spoken to me. I felt as if I were before the god Amon-Ra himself. I dared not look her in the face but stared at her jeweled sandals. I waited in the heavy silence, my heart pounding, frantically trying to understand what the Pharaoh could possibly want of me.

"You do not resemble your uncle," she said finally. I did not answer. Was I meant to answer?

"You are Meru, Senenmut's nephew?"

I nodded numbly.

"Where is he?" Her voice was sharp, demanding.

"I do not know, O Great One," I whispered hoarsely. "I have not seen him for three days." Those are the words I said, but my thoughts were wildly elsewhere. My uncle was missing? He had left without telling the Pharaoh?

Why? Where did he go?

"He did not confide secrets to you?" The voice pressed harder.

I gasped. Did she know I had been shown what should not be seen?

"He did," I murmured.

"What secrets?"

I could not betray my uncle, but I had to answer the Pharaoh. "Nothing about leaving, Divine One," I said. "Nothing about secret plots or plans. Only his deep wish to serve Your Radiance in this life — and beyond."

"I see." And in her voice I heard that she did see, she understood. "You may go then, but if you learn anything about where your uncle is or may be, you will inform me at once."

After my meeting with the Pharaoh, the palace swirled with rumors. The Pharaoh's favorite had vanished. Was he the victim of an evil spell? Had he gone on a mysterious journey? It was so sudden and strange, it made no sense.

It has been weeks now since I was called before the Pharaoh and still there is no sign of Senenmut. I am certain he did not go on a journey. His servants would have known of such plans and nothing is missing from his rooms. No, I fear he is dead, and his body has been hidden or destroyed as a second death. Without a proper burial, his ka has no place to go, an end with no ending.

I close the silver book and look at Adom. This is as much as Meru wrote. The end of the manuscript is the lack of an ending to Senenmut's story. It's exactly what I've been suspecting since we were in Senenmut's tomb—there was no mummy because there was no body. Someone made sure that Senenmut would die not only in this life, but in the next as well. Whoever killed him destroyed his corpse, so his *ka* would have no place to go and would drift forever in nothingness. Hatshepsut didn't exile him in a jealous fit or because of anger over Neferure's death. He was murdered. And the ring pointed to his killer.

"That doesn't sound good for Senenmut," Adom says softly. "Are you supposed to solve his murder? Are you supposed to figure out who killed him and what happened to his body?"

I nod. "I think that's what Hatshepsut wants. But what can I do beyond suspect someone? It's hard to dust for fingerprints that are thousands of years old. How can I prove anything by myself?"

"You're not on your own," Adom says. "There's the old woman who gave you the model of the temple and whoever made sure you found this book and the statue and the ring, all the Servants of Hatshepsut. You have lots of help. "He curls his fingers around mine. "And you have me. That counts for something."

"Yes," I agree. "That counts for a lot. And since you have such a good memory for hieroglyphs, what about the one for Hapuseneb? When Rashid pointed it out in the tomb, I was sure I'd seen it before."

"Do you have a picture of it? I don't remember it looking familiar." Adom shrugs.

"I drew it—here, look." I open my sketchbook and show him the cartouche. "There's a foot and a chick in it, plus a wavy line, a small square, and a hook."

Adom frowns in concentration. "Nope," he finally says. "I don't know it. But I'll keep my eyes open. I'll figure it out for you, I promise."

"I could have seen it that first day in the museum.

We've seen so much in the past few days." Images jostle in my memory—the ruby-eyed snake, the Hatshepsut-faced sphinx, Hapuseneb's soul being weighed, Neferure held by Senenmut. It's too much to think about. I need a break from ancient Egypt, at least for a little while.

Water

THERE DOESN'T SEEM TO BE MUCH WE CAN do to solve the mystery from the hotel, so we decide to relax by the pool. It's still warm enough to swim, and part of me hopes the strange old woman will appear again with another clue, something new to point us in the right direction. The other part wants nothing to happen, so I can spend time with Adom, just have an ordinary day together to make up for hurting his feelings and keeping secrets from him.

It feels good to stretch out in the water. I swim a few laps, then play Marco Polo with Adom until even he has had enough. I dry myself in the late afternoon sun. The shadows are long and the day is turning into chilly evening. We'll have to go in soon, but for now the breeze feels good on my skin. I watch sleepily as Adom turns somersaults and walks on his hands, doing water gymnastics. There is no one else around. Everyone else left with the first cool breeze. There's no one at the bar even. No one with an interesting carving or scrap of papyrus to offer me. It's a normal afternoon at a hotel pool, just like I wanted.

Then Adom dives into the deep end and the splash erupts a sharp panic from deep inside of me.

"Adom!" I scream, terrified. "Are you okay?" I jump into the pool and swim quickly over to him.

"What? What?" he asks, spurting water out of his mouth. "What's the matter? I just dived, that's all. I was in the deep end—it was perfectly safe."

I feel like an idiot. "Of course. I know. You didn't do anything wrong. I just . . . I don't know." I swim to the steps and climb out of the pool. Adom follows me, worried. Shivering, I wrap myself in a towel. "It was really weird. That splash just scared me. It was like a signal that something very bad was happening." I can't explain it any better but I know that something is wrong. Maybe not now, maybe not here at this pool, but some other time, somewhere else, the fall of a body into water was a deadly thing. Suddenly, I know how Senenmut must have died—he drowned in the Nile and that's why there was no body to mummify. He drowned and was eaten by crocodiles. The sudden splash filled me with that horrible certainty.

That night I have another nightmare. I'm back in Hapuseneb's tomb and once again the carvings on the wall writhe and mock me. I can see the name cartouche clearly now, the hieroglyphs seared in deep red on the walls: a leg topped by a wavy line, a flail, a chick, then a square under two chevrons. The symbols expand, growing bigger and bolder until the entire cartouche is filled with red, the name turned into a puddle of blood. I hear the same evil laughter I heard during the day, louder and louder until it stops and there is an abrupt, heavy silence. Hapuseneb's mummy sits up in his sarcophagus. His bony head scans the chamber and stops when it finds me. "You!" he hisses. "You cannot touch me—I curse you! I curse you and the generations after you. I should not be punished. I should be rewarded in the Field of Reeds. I have done nothing wrong, nothing! NOTHING!" The crocodile-headed demon painted on the wall, the one near the weighing of the heart, roars at this last "nothing" and leaps off the wall. In one bound, the monster reaches the mummy and swallows it in its massive jaws. There is no more laughter, just piercing howls of agony.

I wake up, sweating, my own heart pounding furiously. I know why Hapuseneb's heart is so heavy and black. He must be the one who murdered Senenmut, the one who made sure his body was destroyed. His jealousy and hunger for more power pushed him to murder, to sacrifice his place in the afterworld in order to condemn Senenmut.

I drink some water from the glass I left on the bedside table and try to relax. Okay, I tell myself, you think you know what happened to Senenmut. What are you supposed to do with this theory? How does it help Hatshepsut to know what happened to her lover? How does it help Senenmut? And what does any of this have to do with Mom? What am I supposed to get out of all this? What kind of connection do I need to make?

I look over at Adom, asleep in his bed. He never has nightmares. I wish I could sleep as easily and soundly as he does. I listen to his breathing and try to slow mine to match his. Somehow that calms me down and I drift off to sleep, this time until morning, with no dreams at all.

Rashid meets us at breakfast. I try to be friendly,

because now the end of dealing with Mr. Creepy is finally in sight. We have one more day together and then Dad will be here. Actually, his train is supposed to arrive tonight, so we might even see him before we go to bed.

"I am sorry about yesterday," Rashid begins. "But I am sure an afternoon by the pool did not harm you too much."

"We had fun," I agree. "And you've been very generous with your time. We don't want to impose anymore. We can go to the Valley of the Kings on our own today. I'm sure the hotel can tell us how to manage."

"I will not hear of it!" Rashid is appalled by the idea. "What would your father say? No! This is not something for you to 'manage.' It is an honor for me to escort you. And," he leans forward, his fingers spread on the table, and winks at Adom, "you will learn much more with me as your guide."

The light glitters on his heavy ring, catching my eye. Suddenly I realize where I've seen the same hieroglyph before—it's Hapuseneb's name cartouche, the one I copied down in his tomb. There it is on the ring Rashid wears! I was right—it's an ancient artifact, probably taken from the vizier's tomb. No wonder Rashid has always seemed creepy to me. The last thing I want to do is spend another day with him, tainted as he is by Hapuseneb's ugly soul.

"You're too kind," I protest. "We've bothered you enough." But no matter what I say, Rashid is just as insistent. There's no way out. We'll have to spend yet more time with Rashid. We're one big happy family on our way to the western bank of the Nile, back to the land of the setting sun, the home of the dead.

I don't get a chance to share my discovery with Adom until we're in the jeep on the West Bank, driving toward the Valley of the Kings. Rashid sits next to the driver as usual. Muffled by the roar of the engine, I tell Adom about the ring, how I'm sure it's really Hapuseneb's, not some tourist copy.

"So what?" Adom yells into my ear. "Okay, he's stealing from a tomb, but he discovered it. Maybe he thinks it's like a finder's fee, something he earned. And if there's a mummy's curse on it, then he's the one who will suffer, so what's the worry?"

I shake my head. "It's not the theft that bugs me—it's like it's a direct link to Hapuseneb. And Hapuseneb was a bad person, I know it!"

There isn't time for more discussion. The driver pulls up next to a big tour bus. We're seeing more royal tombs, this time of kings, not queens, but the tomb I really want to see, Hatshepsut's, isn't open to the public, and even Mr. Very Important Rashid can't get us in. As beautiful as the tombs are, I'm too distracted to appreciate them. My eyes keep staring at Hapuseneb's ring, as if I expect it to burst into sulfurous flames any second. My skin crawls just being near Rashid, but I have to admit he's a perfect host. He's extra patient with Adom, clearly trying to make up for the curtness of yesterday, and even offers to buy Adom a souvenir after we visit the last tomb, stopping at the row of makeshift stands near the entry road to the Valley of the Kings. Adom finally selects a polished blue stone egg, something not particularly Egyptian or ancient looking, the kind of thing you could pick up anywhere.

"Why did you choose that?" I ask him as we drive back to the shore for the ferry ride across the Nile.

"It's pretty," Adom says. "I like the color. And it feels good in my hand."

"But you can find stone eggs like that anywhere," I object.

"Only I didn't. I found it here." Adom puts the egg in his pants pocket, away from my disapproving eyes.

"You can choose something as well," Rashid suggests. "Consider it my farewell gift to you, since your father arrives tonight." He puts his hand on my arm. I flinch from the searing coldness of the ring.

"That's kind of you," I force myself to say, "but I'm fine. I don't want anything." Except to get far away from you, I add in my head.

Rashid doesn't press the point. Everyone's quiet and tired on the boat ride back. It's been a long, full day, the sun is setting, and my head is swirling with images from my dream last night, the bleeding name cartouche, Rashid's ring, and the tomb paintings we saw today, rows of jackal-headed gods striding through eternity, coiled cobras next to cattle next to dancers next to piles of fish, all painted in bright colors.

I don't even notice the other boat until it's much too close. The man guiding our small, flat boat tries to steer clear of the bigger speedboat, but he can't move quickly enough. The speedboat jolts into the back of us, tipping the boat dangerously. Adom falls to the floor in the center, Rashid tumbles next to him, but I'm in the back of the boat and am pulled the other way, flipping out of the boat into the dark river water. I gulp for air, then feel myself yanked down, as if iron hands are gripping my ankles and pulling me to the bottom of the Nile. I can hear the same evil laugh from Hapuseneb's tomb and the mummy's face flashes in front of my eyes. I tell myself I'm imagining all this, but I'm filled with the same terror that hit me when Adom dived into the pool. This is a place of death and I'm meant to drown. I know it. But I don't accept it. I thrash my legs, fighting wildly to free myself, pushing myself up for air, only to be pulled back down again and again.

Finally something shifts in the water, the evil laugh trickles away, and the heavy weights around my ankles vanish. I break the surface, gulping. My lungs ache and my legs are exhausted. I tread water, trying to find our boat, but I don't see it anywhere. How long have I been struggling? Luckily I'm a strong swimmer, and it doesn't take long for me to stroke back to the eastern shore. I stumble through the muck and reeds when the river gets too shallow to swim anymore. I'm almost on dry land when I fall back into the mud. My hands sink into the thick clay and when I pull them free, I'm holding something small and hard. Before I rinse it in the water, I know what it is—a ring, the twin of the one I found in Hapuseneb's tomb. I shudder with cold or dread, I'm not sure which. Is this the ring Senenmut was wearing when he drowned? Is this my proof of how he died, or just another weird coincidence?

17

The Eighteenth Dynasty

I DON'T RECOGNIZE THE PART OF THE SHORE I've waded onto. The mummy museum and tacky souvenir stands must be to the south or north. All I see here are reeds and mud. I scan the shore, trying to find some kind of landmark. A collection of mud huts lies directly to the east. To the north I see more huts, and to the south, the same. How could I have ended up so far from the dock at Luxor? Adom will be worried that I'm lost, and actually I'm not sure where I am. I'll just have to chance on a direction. I head south, clutching the ring tightly in my hand. My wet clothes feel good in the heat.

My clothes? I'm not wearing my jeans and T-shirt

anymore. Instead, I have on a thin cotton dress. My sneakers are gone, replaced with sandals. And the day was warm before, but now it's scorching. What is going on?

That's when I notice that the sun is high in the sky. Just a little while ago, it was setting. Something's very strange. I'm not where I should be, I'm wearing strange clothes, and time is all messed up.

I hear voices ahead and hurry to catch up to them. Three boys are arguing heatedly, but they're not dressed in jeans or shorts or the Egyptian galabeyah. They look like actors in an ancient Egyptian play, wearing short white skirts, sandals, and nothing else. My stomach tightens when I see them. One of them looks very familiar. He turns to face me and stops midsentence. The other two follow his gaze and also look shocked, panicked actually. After a long, frozen moment, the two boys turn and run, leaving the familiar one alone with me.

"Neferure?" His voice quavers and his accent is strange. He drops to his knees and bows his head.

I shake my head. "No," I say. "I'm Talibah. Can you tell me how to get to Luxor temple?" I figure from there I can find my way back to the hotel.

The boy looks up at me, his eyes wide with wonder.

He reminds me of Adom. Maybe that's why I think

I've seen him before. His chin and eyes are just like my brother's. He even has the same narrow shoulders and slender neck. And the ears—the exact same ears! I know most people don't notice ears. After all, they're not especially cute or attractive. But I know Adom's ears very well—they're small, but not too small, and fit neatly against his head. When he was little, I could get him to go to sleep by stroking his ears. It kind of hypnotized him somehow. So I know his ears. And here they are, on this strange boy.

I smile at him, trying to reassure him. He looks like he's deciding whether I'm the good kind of stranger or the bad kind, someone he can talk to or should run away from.

"It's okay," I say gently. "I'm not going to hurt you. I just need your help. I'm lost and I don't know how to get back to Luxor. Or if you know the way to Karnak, I can find my way from there." I wish I could speak Arabic. I can't tell if he understands anything I'm saying.

"Luxor?" I repeat. "Or Karnak?"

"Karnak!" the boy says. He quivers with excitement. "Karnak, Neferure!" He jabbers a stream of words that make no sense to me, but at least we both agree on Karnak. It's the one word we have in common. He starts to walk away, heading in the direction I came from.

He turns back and sees me hesitating. Then he runs to me and shyly takes my hand, leading me along. I don't want to let go of him, but he's got me by the hand that's holding the ring and I'm afraid I'll drop it.

"Wait," I say, and shift to hold him with the other hand. As I do, he notices the ring and before I can stop him, he's plucked it from my palm.

He stares at the ring, his eyes filling with tears. I can only make out three words from what he says, all names—Senenmut, Hapuseneb, and Neferure. I wish I could understand him.

"Yes, Senenmut," I repeat. "It's Senenmut's ring."

The boy nods, the tears now streaking down his dusty cheeks. He clutches the ring and starts to run. He doesn't seem like a thief, but I don't know how else to explain what he's doing. I chase after him, yelling at him to stop.

He's loping steadily, not running away, and every now and then, he looks back to make sure I'm still following. We come to the edge of a village and dodge through goats and sheep. This doesn't seem like the right way to Karnak, but I keep the boy in my sight, even though I have no idea where he's leading me.

We wind down narrow dirt streets lined with white-washed mud buildings. I still can't get my bearings. Donkeys, carts, goats, and people crowd around us, adding to the confusion. There are no Internet cafés, no souvenir stands, though people pass by carrying platters stacked with fresh flat bread. My stomach growls and I realize I'm hungry, but there's no time to stop and buy anything. I'm afraid that if I take my eyes off the boy, I'll lose him in the maze of streets.

Then the maze opens out onto a beautiful garden crisscrossed by streams. Colorful birds flit from tree to tree. Children race past, laughing and playing. They look like something out of an ancient Egyptian wall painting—dark eyes rimmed with eyeliner, heads shaved except for a ponytail on one side, clothed in white skirts and sandals.

The boy finally stops at the end of the garden, before a high wooden gate flanked by guards. I don't mean the usual guards you see in Egypt, dressed in khaki uniforms with old machine guns strapped around their shoulders. These guards hold spears and wear the same skirts and sandals as most of the people I've seen. They have gold cuffs around their wrists and blue-and-silver beads in wide collars around their necks. It's as if

I've stumbled onto a movie set. This is getting weirder and weirder.

The boy bows and says something to the guards. The one on the left nods and swings open the tall gate. The boy strides through, chin high with confidence. I hesitate, but what else can I do? I follow the boy into another garden, more beautiful than the first, with fountains and elaborate mosaic walkways, through a courtyard, down a great hall. The walls are brightly painted, like at Hatshepsut's temple, but here there are no scrapes or gouges. All the lines and colors are as fresh as if they'd been finished yesterday. It's like a Disneyland version of the real thing, perfectly restored. We come to another room flanked by guards like the ones outside. Again the boy says something and is allowed in. He gestures at me to follow.

Then it hits me. I do know him. I've pictured him looking just like this as I read his book. He's Meru.

Suddenly it all makes sense—a crazy kind of sense, a dreaming kind of sense. I must be asleep, and in my dream, I'm back in the Eighteenth Dynasty—in the time of Hatshepsut, Senenmut, Neferure, and Meru. Only Senenmut is already dead, which is why seeing his ring made Meru cry. And Neferure is dead, too, but I must look a lot like her. Maybe Meru even thinks I'm her spirit come back to haunt the home she was torn from far too young. I'm not surprised when Meru leads me into an elaborate room. Its high ceiling is painted with eagles spreading their wings in rich, deep blues. The columns along the walls are like tall redwood trees, the statues next to them are giants. It's the most impressive place I've ever seen. At the opposite end, there's a low platform with a chair. I know it's not an ordinary chair, though it's carved from wood and not especially fancy. It's a throne. Sitting on it is Egypt's only woman pharaoh, Hatshepsut. She's slight and elegant with finely chiseled features, and definitely a woman, wearing a sheer dress, a heavy wig, and lots of jewelry. But there's a forcefulness that vibrates from her, an intensity to her eyes that make her seem like a pharaoh first, a woman second.

Meru drops to his knees and touches his forehead to the floor. I copy his gesture. Even though I know this is only a dream, I don't want to offend Hatshepsut. It feels like a real honor to be before her, not an imaginary one.

I'm staring at the ground, waiting for what comes next. I hear Hatshepsut speak, her voice dark and commanding. My heart beats wildly—it's the voice from my dream! I tell myself to calm down. Of course it's the voice from my dream, since I'm dreaming again. Naturally the voices would match. My subconscious isn't stupid, after all.

Meru answers Hatshepsut. He sits up, rocking back on his heels, and holds out the ring to show her. Again I hear the names Senenmut, Hapuseneb, and Neferure.

When Hatshepsut speaks, her voice is flinty and cold. She grabs the ring from Meru and barks something to the servants standing behind her. Then she does something amazing. She gets off of her throne, kneels before me, and lifts my chin up, cupping my face in her hands.

"Neferure," she sighs. She's trying not to cry, but the tears escape and run silently down her cheeks. She doesn't speak, but I can hear her voice in my head, the voice from my dreams. "I knew you would find him. I knew you would find the truth. Now I can rest."

I stare at her, not knowing what to say. Now that she's closer to me, more of a person and less of a distant ruler, her face is achingly familiar. Her almond eyes, her broad brow, her long nose—it's Mom's face. Now I'm the one who's holding back tears.

There's a flurry of motion, and a short bald man strides in, followed by a small flock of servants. He bows to Hatshepsut, who quickly moves back to her throne.

She's the regal pharaoh again. Meru and I watch silently as she yells angrily at the bald man. I hear the name Hapuseneb over and over again, along with an occasional "Senenmut." Then Hatshepsut throws Senenmut's ring down angrily at the bald man's feet. He picks it up, not at all upset by the pharaoh's temper. He stands there, waiting for her to finish. Then he starts talking, calmly, deliberately, gesturing with the ring. He turns to Meru and glares, then notices my existence for the first time. He sputters, his eyes wide, as if he'd just seen a ghost. He looks absolutely terrified.

Hatshepsut roars at him to leave. At least I think that's what she yelled, because the bald man walks out of the room as fast as he can without breaking into a run. He's still gripping the ring, but Hatshepsut doesn't seem to care. She looks at me again, and her voice softens. I don't know what she's saying, but her tone is warm and full of love and that's enough for me.

Then she says something to Meru, who bows down again, then takes my hand. He pulls me back to the door. I don't want to leave Hatshepsut, but I know, even in my dream, that I don't belong here. I need to get home, so I retrace my steps with him, out of the audience room, down the hall, through the courtyard and gardens to the main gate. Again, the guards open the gates. I step through them.

But the garden is gone. The crowded streets, the whitewashed houses, the goats, the donkeys, the people have all vanished. I'm back on the shore of the Nile, the sun dipping into the horizon. I shiver, chilled by my suddenly wet clothes. The thin cotton dress dried long ago but when I look down, the dress is gone. I'm back in my T-shirt and jeans. My soggy sneakers are back on my feet. I'm cold, it's getting dark, and I still need to find my way home. I wish I would just wake up. I look downstream and see a dock reaching into the water. I walk to it in the quickly dimming light. The sun has almost set, but the streetlights aren't yet on. Streetlights? I hear a car drive by and recognize the line of souvenir shops across the street. And there, farther down the road, I can make out the sign for the mummy museum. I'm back in Luxor. This is so weird—I'm awake without waking up. At least, I think I'm awake. I pinch my arm. I can definitely feel it, but I felt the hot sun before, the cool stone floor in Hatshepsut's audience hall and the warmth of her breath in my ear. Was I ever asleep?

IX

The Twenty–first Century

B Y THE TIME I GET BACK TO THE HOTEL, I'M more confused than ever. When I found the ring, had I found Senenmut? Does this mean the strange dreams, the voice, the statues speaking to me, all that won't happen again? Is the mystery over? It doesn't feel like a real ending to me. It's somehow disappointing.

Adom is waiting in the lobby and jumps up to hug me.

"I was so worried! We looked for you everywhere! You just disappeared!" He starts to cry. "I was scared, so scared!"

"Shhh," I soothe, holding him tightly. "I was scared, too, but everything's okay now. I'm fine—tired, but fine."

"Don't ever do that again," Adom says, burrowing back into me, not caring that his clothes are damp now, too. "You're always getting lost."

I'm about to protest that I wasn't lost, but this time I really was. I still don't know where I was or how I got back. I can't make sense of anything.

"Where's Rashid?" I say instead. "He left you here by yourself?"

"I told him to. He needed to go to the police station to file a report. He wanted them to send out boats to search for you. He's probably with them."

"I guess we'd better let him know I'm okay. But can I take a hot bath and get into some clean, dry clothes first?" I ask.

"I'll call him while you take a bath," Adom offers. "He gave me his cell phone number, because he didn't like to leave me alone."

"Good idea," I agree, relieved I don't have to talk to Rashid myself. What would I say when he asked where I'd been?

Adom pulls me by the hand to the elevator. He glances around, then whispers, "And don't worry about all your secret stuff. I took good care of your backpack. It's safe in the room."

I smile at his dramatic gestures. "Thank you," I whisper back. I follow Adom to our room. Looking at the back of his neck, the set of his shoulders, his ears, I'm reminded of Meru. Was that boy really Meru? Why did he look so much like my brother? Why did everyone call me Neferure? Who was the bald man and why did Hatshepsut throw Senenmut's ring at him?

I wish I could turn my brain off. Soaking in the hot water feels so comforting, and I let my thoughts drift. It's strange to think that I was submerged in water in a very different way a short while ago, not soothing at all then, but terrifying. I think about what happened, how quickly the day changed into a nightmare. Where did the speedboat come from, I wonder. It doesn't matter, I decide. One way or another, I was meant to fall into the Nile. Somehow that's part of my destiny.

And once I was in the water, something else happened, something creepy and supernatural. Those hands gripping me and pulling me down weren't human, I know that. Something else, some evil spirit, was trying to drown me. Could it have been Senenmut's disturbed *ka*, wanting to inflict the same fate it suffered on anyone unlucky enough to fall into the river where he drowned? Or was it Hapuseneb's spirit, doomed to haunt the place where it committed its horrible crime? I remember the nightmare when Hapuseneb cursed me. Was this part of the curse, to die by drowning?

I hear Hapuseneb's words again and a shiver runs through me. Now I recognize the voice. He was the bald man! I think back over what happened. Meru calls me Neferure. He knows the signet ring is Senenmut's. If he saw Neferure coming out of the Nile where Senenmut drowned, holding his ring, what would the boy assume? He would think Neferure's spirit was proving to him how the architect had died. He would see it as a message from the afterlife. So he leads the spirit to Hatshepsut, shows the ring to the pharoah, and explains how he found it and what must have happened to Senenmut. That would explain why Hatshepsut calls for the high priest and confronts him. Hapuseneb denies it, and she throws Senenmut's ring at him. Maybe she tells him he's earned it. Maybe she curses him with it. Even if I really was there, watching it all, I'll never know, since I couldn't understand either of them. I could only understand Hatshepsut that one time when it was the dream voice echoing in my head.

There's a knock on the bathroom door. "Yes?" I call out. "What is it?"

"I talked to Rashid," Adom yells. "He's coming over to check on us. I told him we're fine, but he wants to see for himself. I think he's really worried something bad could've happened to us and Dad would be furious at him."

The last person I want to see right now is Rashid, but I dry myself off and get dressed in pajamas and a robe. Maybe if I look like I'm ready to go to bed, he won't stay long. He can reassure himself we're fine, then be on his way.

The visit is as quick as I'd hoped. There's a knock at the door, Rashid pokes his head in, sees I'm still alive, with all my arms and legs, sighs in relief, and turns to go. "Thank Allah, all is well," he says.

When I'm sure he has really left, I sit on the bed next to Adom. "I have a lot to tell you, and I'm not sure if you'll believe me."

"Of course I will," Adom promises. "Just talk."

So I do. I start with the ghostly hands pulling me down in the water and end with Hatshepsut throwing the ring at Hapuseneb. "Then I walked out of the palace and as soon as I left the main gate, I was back here. I mean, not here in this hotel, but here in this time and place, back by the dock at Luxor."

Adom is concentrating so hard he looks like he's studying for a math test.

"I don't know if what happened to you was real or a dream, but the stuff in your backpack is absolutely real." He reaches for my bag and unzips it, taking out the stone carvings carefully. He lines up on the bedside table the model of the temple next to the miniature Senenmut. Then he digs around until he finds the ring and places it between the sculptures.

I reach for the ring. As my fingers close on it, I see Hatshepsut once again, yelling at Hapuseneb and throwing the ring at him. I see him pick it up and walk away, proud of the trophy in his grasp. The columned room swirls around me and I'm so dizzy, I drop the ring.

"What's the matter?" Adom presses his face close to mine. "Are you okay? You look like you just saw a ghost!"

"I did," I say. "Two of them—Hatshepsut and Hapuseneb." I look at the ring, glinting in the carpet. "I just had the weirdest idea. After Senenmut drowned, somehow his ring washed up on the shore of the Nile, where I found it. I brought it to Hatshepsut. She threw it at Hapuseneb. He took it away and later, when he died, had it buried in his tomb with him, where I found it again."

"That's crazy! You act like you've been alive in two different time periods." Adom picks up the ring and sets it back on the night table.

"How else could I find the same ring twice, in completely different places? Somehow I'm part of all this. I'm the one who gives Hatshepsut the proof Senenmut is dead. Without the ring, she'd never have known. She told me so herself. She said I'd found him. And it's because I look like Neferure, the ghost of her dead daughter."

"You didn't tell me that part before. Hatshepsut talked to you?" Adom stares at me like I'm the ghost.

"I forgot that part." I try to fill in anything I left out, but it's hard for me to make sense of it all, much less explain it as a logical story to someone else.

Adom struggles to take it all in. "So the mystery is all solved now? It feels as mysterious as ever to me." Adom turns the ring thoughtfully between his fingers. "Let's start from what we know, okay? We know that Senenmut was killed and his body destroyed. There are two questions: Who murdered him, and how? The rings must be part of the answer."

"Exactly." I wait to see if Adom will come to the same conclusion I have.

"And your falling into the water is another clue." Adom's voice pitches up in excitement. "Because that's how Senenmut was killed—he was pushed into the water, too—only he drowned. Maybe he didn't know how to swim, or maybe his arms and legs were tied so he couldn't. Anyway, he drowned. That would take care of getting rid of his body."

I nod. "That's what I think, too."

"And," Adom continues, "the ring from Hapuseneb's tomb obviously points to the murderer. How else would he have gotten something so important to Senenmut? Plus, the high priest had a motive—jealousy. He didn't like sharing power with anyone, especially a commoner like Senenmut. He hated the architect and spread mean rumors about him, trying to get him away from Hatshepsut. When that didn't work, maybe he decided to take more drastic steps. He sounds like he could commit that kind of crime. And he would be in the palace, the same as Senenmut, so he could easily find the opportunity. It all fits!"

"That theory works. But what about the rest of it? Why are we part of this whole thing? And what does it mean that I look like Neferure and you look like Meru?" I take out my sketchbook and quickly draw what I remember of Meru's face. "See?" I show Adom the portrait.

"I look like Meru? That's another thing you didn't tell me." Adom grabs the sketchbook and narrows his eyes. "What else did you conveniently forget to mention?"

"Nothing!" I say. "Now you know everything." But I haven't told him about the nightmare where Hapuseneb curses me. I haven't told him what I saw in the priest's tomb. It all seems so crazy. Anyway, he knows plenty. He doesn't need to hear every little detail of my imagination. At least, I hope it's my imagination.

Adom looks like he's trying to decide whether to believe me or not. I'm relieved when he lets it drop. "It's a good thing Dad's coming tonight," he says. "We have to tell him all this. He might know the answers."

It's like Dad is already part of the conversation, because just then the phone rings and it's him, saying he's getting in late, we should go to sleep, and he'll see us in the morning.

"Okay, Dad," I tell him. "We miss you. We have a lot to tell you."

"I miss you, too," he says. "And I'm sure with all you've seen these last few days, you have a lot of interesting news."

He has no idea.

The Seeker

THERE'S A KNOCK ON THE DOOR EARLY IN the morning while I'm getting dressed in the bathroom. Adom's awake and he runs to open it.

"Dad!" I hear him yell.

"Adom!" It's Dad's familiar baritone. I quickly shove my legs into my jeans and hurry into the room.

"Talibah!" Dad lets go of Adom and turns to hug me. He looks rumpled and tired, as if he just got off the train this morning instead of last night. The circles under his eyes are darker than usual, his full lips soft and sad. I wonder if it's hard for him to be back here, in Egypt, without Mom. But I can't think about that for long.

"Dad, we have so much to tell you! You won't

believe it!" Adom is so excited, he doesn't know where to begin. "You tell him, Talibah. Tell him everything that's happened."

Dad smiles. "I'm glad you've had a chance to see so much. Tell me, how do you like the tombs in the Valley of the Kings? Have you been to Hatshepsut's temple?"

I nod. "Yes, but that's not what we need to talk to you about."

Dad sits down on Adom's rumpled bed. "Has there been a problem? Was your wallet stolen? Did you lose your passport?"

"No," I say, "nothing like that." I sit across from Dad on my bed. I have no idea how to start, but somehow the words tumble out without my thinking about what to say. I start with the old woman and her strange gift. I show Dad the model of the temple and then describe my dream. As I hand Dad each of the gifts I've found, he studies them carefully, but doesn't interrupt me. He listens intently all the way to the end, to yesterday when I fell into the Nile and found Senenmut's ring.

I've talked for so long, my throat is dry. I gulp down some water and wait to see what Dad will say. Does he think I'm crazy?

Dad examines the ring closely. "You know, of course, that you must return this to Hapuseneb's tomb."

I nod. I wasn't planning to—it doesn't seem like the right resting place for Senenmut—but now that I've shown it to Dad and admitted where I found it, I guess I don't have a choice. I look at Adom. Somehow when we came up with our theory, it seemed more plausible. With Dad, it comes off as complete fantasy.

"But Dad," Adom says, "what about finding Senenmut? How can we help him now when he's been dead for thousands of years? How can we give his spirit peace? And how come this all happened to us in the first place? Why do some people call Talibah Neferure?"

Dad sighs. It's early in the morning, but he looks very tired, like a heavy weight has been placed on him.

"I need to think, Adom. This is all very serious, more serious than you know."

"Then you don't think I'm nuts?" I ask. "You're not mad at me?"

Dad gently strokes my cheek, something he's never done before. "No, my Talibah, you are not crazy, not at all, and I'm not mad at you. One thing I can tell you, you have lived up to your name, just as your mother said you would."

I'm startled. "What do you mean? What does my name have to do with this?"

"Talibah means 'seeker of truth.' When you were born, your mother held you in her arms and looked down at your small face and she said that is what you would be. She said, 'My daughter will find the truth. She will make the family whole again. That is the name she must carry, Seeker of Truth—Talibah.' She insisted you would solve some ancient mystery, bring healing to a wound that was thousands of years old. I didn't take that part seriously, but I agreed to the name. She was so sure, there was no arguing with her."

"Didn't you ask what truth I was supposed to find? What did Mom mean?" I think the mystery is becoming more confusing, not less.

"Yes, I asked what she meant, but she said that wasn't for me to know. It had something to do with her ancestors. I admit I was hurt that she was choosing a name that had nothing to do with me, that I had no say in, but she was firm. You were Talibah—for her reasons—and I accepted that."

"Is it her voice I hear in the dreams, not Hatshepsut's?" I ask. "Is she the one asking me to find Senenmut?"

Dad shakes his head sadly. "How can I know? All I

can tell you is that I believe you. You were asked to do a special task, to find the truth that your mother knew you would find. I can't say how that makes the family whole again, but I remember that's what she said, something like that."

Suddenly Dad grabs my arm, pulling me to him. "Where did you get that?" he asks sharply.

"The bracelet?" I ask, surprised by his tone. He said he wasn't angry with me, but he sure seems mad.

"Yes, that bracelet." Dad holds up my wrist to examine it closely.

"I gave it to her," Adom interrupts. "I bought it at the market when Rashid took me."

Dad drops my hand and stares at Adom. "You bought this? You found this? Where? What market?"

Adom is as taken aback by Dad's intensity as I am. "You know, at one of those stands people set up in the bazaar in Luxor. I don't remember exactly which one, but Rashid can show you. "

"What's the big deal?" I ask. "It's a nice bracelet. Adom didn't steal it. He paid for it."

Dad slumps forward, holding his face in his hands. I watch his back and shoulders shudder and realize with horror that he's crying. Adom and I exchange looks.

What's going on here? I haven't seen Dad cry since Mom's funeral. Why the tears now?

Slowly the sobs subside and Dad straightens up, looking at us with reddened eyes.

"I'm sorry," he rasps. "That bracelet is the same one your mother had. It was a family heirloom, passed on for generations. She was planning to give it to you, Talibah, when you turned sixteen. But when our house was robbed the year after she died, it was stolen. I thought I'd never see it again, but here it is."

"The exact same bracelet?" I stare at the silver band with the scarab amulet. "You mean it's like the one Mom had. It can't be the same one."

"No." Dad shakes his head. "I know it seems impossible, but this is her bracelet. See that nick on the left side of the scarab's head? And the way the clasp of the locket is dented? How could two different bracelets have the exact same wear and tear? And what's inside the locket?" Dad closes his eyes as if he's afraid of the answer.

"Nothing," I say as I swing open the locket. "It's empty. What was in Mom's?"

Dad sighs. "Well, that's been lost, but the bracelet remains."

"What, what's been lost? What was in there?" Adom asks. "Was it very valuable?"

"It wasn't valuable at all, but it was important to your mother. It was a piece of paper with something written on it that she said would help Talibah in her search. I don't know what it said, because I only saw the rolled-up papyrus inside the scarab. I wasn't allowed to read it."

I trace the scarab lightly with my finger. I didn't know that Mom had left me anything. I wish I had the paper she'd meant for me. I wish I knew if I was doing what she wanted me to do. I feel lost. I look at Dad, but now his presence doesn't comfort me. Instead I'm angry, a slow, building rage rising up from the pit of my stomach.

"When were you going to tell me all this!" I roar. "You never talk about Mom—never! You've kept this all from me, like some kind of secret. Well, it *is* a secret, but one between Mom and me, not you and her!"

"I was going to tell you." Dad keeps his voice calm. "The time just wasn't right yet. I wasn't ready yet."

"Would the time ever be right? And what were you going to say? Sorry, the family heirloom your mother meant for you has been stolen and P.S. your name had a special meaning for her?"

"Come now, Talibah, be fair," Dad protests. "You're right, the secret was between you and her, so what could I really tell you? Some vague sense your mother had about destiny? Why should I burden you with that? Why tell you about a gift you weren't getting?"

"Because," I say, my anger subsiding into tears, "I need to know about Mom, not be protected from her memory. When you don't talk about her, it makes you seem cold, and then I hate you." It's such a relief to say it that I say it again. "I hate you."

Dad pulls me to him, rocking us back and forth the way I remember Mom used to do when I was little and needed comfort. "I'm sorry," he says, kissing the top of my head. "I'm not good at this. I don't know how to keep Mom alive for you and protect myself from the pain of thinking about her at the same time. I can't. I know I should, but I can't."

I want to hold myself hard against him, to keep the ice shard of hate from melting, but I can't. I let my tense muscles relax. I let my father rock me, because his touch is so rare and it feels good to be held. I let myself miss my mother.

Adom squeezes himself between us. He wants to be hugged, too, and we do, both of us encircling him in our arms. We stay that way for a long time, listening to our three beating hearts, until Dad kisses us both and says, "Who's hungry for breakfast besides me?"

20

Darkness

A GOOD, HOT BREAKFAST PUTS EVERYONE in a better mood. By the time Adom's stuffed himself with pancakes and sausage, he's beaming with excitement.

"I'm part of the mystery, too, you know," he says. "I'm the one who found the bracelet! I'm the one who got that gift, that clue, and it's the most important one, because it's from Mom herself!"

I nod. "Yes, you're part of this, too, a very important part." Something strikes me as I say this, that Adom really is central to the mystery, like Meru. "I don't think it's a coincidence that you found the bracelet. It's like Meru finding Senenmut's ring with my help.

Somehow you're connected to Meru—you look just like him."

Adom looks at Dad. "Are we descended from Meru? Is he my great-great-great-great-great-great-a-thousand-times-great-grandfather?"

Dad laughs. "I suppose he could be! You're certainly descended from a long line of Egyptians. And you both have an extraordinary sense of the ancient world. You really didn't need my help with all this. You figured it all out by yourselves."

"But we need you now," I insist. "What good is our theory? And what do Senenmut and Hatshepsut have to do with Mom? What's her connection to all this? What's mine?"

Dad shakes his head. "I don't know, but when you find out her connection, you'll understand yours, that I'm sure of."

There isn't time to puzzle it all out before we have to meet with Rashid. I thought we were done with him, but naturally Dad wants to see Hapuseneb's tomb and he's made me promise to put the ring back exactly where I found it. I don't want to go. The nightmare of the high priest's mummy cursing me is still vivid and so is the vision of the demon devouring Hapuseneb when his evil heart sinks on the scale. Besides, now I know Hapuseneb murdered Senenmut. Walking into his tomb is like entering the dark pit of his poisonous soul.

Adom seems to understand. This time he doesn't eagerly charge ahead with Rashid. After the driver parks the jeep, Adom lets Dad and Rashid go ahead and hangs back with me, holding my hand. I'm hit with overwhelming nausea again as I use the flashlight to show us the way down the corridor to the burial chamber. Adom can tell something's wrong. He slows his pace to match mine.

"What's the matter?" he asks. "You look terrible."

The air tastes bitter and metallic. I can barely choke it down. "It's this place," I whisper. "I hate it here."

"Me, too," Adom whispers back. "Let's go back. We've already seen everything."

"But you thought it was cool. Don't you want to see it again?" I ask, forcing myself forward.

"That was before I knew that Hapuseneb killed Senenmut. This is the home of a murderer and it stinks like one." Adom wrinkles his nose.

"You smell it, too?" I feel weaker and weaker.

"Yes, let's go. This place is bad for you!" Adom starts

to pull me back up the corridor and I'm relieved to turn and follow him.

"Wait!" I say. "The ring. I have to put it back."

"I'll do it," Adom offers. I feel a jolt as he takes the ring and the flashlight, and darts into the murky dark. Dad and Rashid are so far ahead that we can barely see the beam of their flashlight. I stand in the blackness, waiting, my hand throbbing where the ring once touched it.

"You have found him!" It's the urgent voice again, the one from my dreams.

The voice has blown in cool, fresh air, and the nausea leaves me as suddenly as it hit me.

"Mom?" My own voice quavers.

"Daughter and not my daughter. Neferure and not Neferure. You have done well." The voice is softer now, fainter.

"Mom?" I ask again.

There's no answer, only silence. Then the sound of Adom's footsteps as he runs up to me.

"Done! We can go now." He takes my hand and leads me up into the daylight. I'm still turning the words over in my head—"Daughter and not my daughter. Neferure and not Neferure." What do they mean? Was it Mom's voice or not? Was it Hatshepsut's? How can I ever know?

Adom and I crouch in the scrap of shade the jeep provides, waiting for Dad and Rashid to come out. The tomb was a refuge from the sun and heat, but we'd both rather broil than go back inside. I tell Adom about the voice while I sketch the outside of the tomb. There's nothing to do except talk, draw, and sweat.

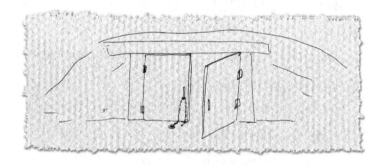

"Does that sound like something Mom would say?" I ask.

"I don't know," Adom says. "I don't even know what it means. Somehow you're Neferure, but you aren't her—I mean, obviously you aren't. You're you, Talibah, so how can you be Neferure, too? But that's what they called you at the pool, remember? That wasn't a mistake, like you thought. It means something."

"I just wish I knew what." I pick up some sand and watch it dribble out of my fist. All the pieces are there, but I don't know how to make sense of them. Mom is the strangest part of all. How does she fit into the mystery? What did she mean about making her family whole again? What is the truth she wanted me to find?

Rashid's driver walks over to us, leaving the corner of shade he found on the other side of the tomb, and offers us some water. "Why are you here, in the heat? You're bored with mummies now?" he teases.

Adom shrugs. "I guess."

The driver tousles Adom's hair, a gesture I know my brother hates and one that is all too common in Egypt. Even strangers passing us on the sidewalk feel free to reach over and pat Adom like a pet. Once he saw a man's hand coming toward him and ducked, leaving the stranger with a handful of air and a puzzled look on his face. This time he shakes the driver off, twisting away from his touch.

"What I'm really bored with is being patted like I'm a neighborhood dog," Adom growls.

"Oh, ho!" chuckles the driver. "I've offended you. You think I'm treating you like a dog, but no, I'm treating you like a boy. I do not mean to insult you."

"I'm not insulted," Adom says. "I just don't want to be touched."

The driver looks surprised and decides to change the

subject by offering to teach us how to play an Egyptian card game. Adom has won twice, the driver four times by the time Dad and Rashid come out of the tomb.

Dad is clearly excited, deep in a discussion with Rashid about the amazing find he's just seen. Rashid is his old, lecturing self again, not the sickly green he was during our last tomb visit. He finishes explaining some particularly arcane detail to Dad, then turns to Adom, flinging his arms out dramatically.

"What happened to you? Last time you were so thrilled to see the tomb, you did not want to leave. I had to drag you away, remember? And this time you barely go in at all. What is wrong?"

Before I can warn him not to say anything, or if he has to answer, to make some lame excuse, Adom does the worst thing possible—he tells the truth.

"That was before I knew who Hapuseneb really was. Now that I know he's a creep, I don't like his tomb. I mean, he murdered Senenmut, and that makes his tomb the home of a murderer's soul. That's not a great place to hang out."

Rashid's eyes flash with rage and his thick brows are drawn down into angry arrows. "How dare you!" he thunders. "How dare you blacken the high priest's name! Hapuseneb's soul was pure and good. He was a man of honor and great spiritual power. Senenmut was the one with the small soul. He was of common birth and did not deserve the power and status the pharaoh gave him. He took advantage of her, used her to get his own way."

"Senenmut wasn't like that!" I protest, putting my arm protectively around Adom, trying to shield him from Rashid, who looks capable of spitting shards of glass, he's so mad. "You've got it all backward—Senenmut was the honorable, spiritual one. Hapuseneb was the one with the small, shriveled, evil fist of a soul. He's the one whose heart was so heavy, a demon ate him when he passed to the afterlife. You're not excavating the tomb of a great man. It's the tomb of a jealous, bitter murderer!"

"NO!" Rashid roars. He lunges forward to grab me, but Dad pulls us behind him, so Rashid ends up with a handful of Dad's shirt.

I've never seen Dad so angry. His face is almost purple and the veins in his neck are bulging. He clamps his hand around Rashid's wrist and twists it away.

"Rashid," he says, biting off the words, "you will NOT touch my children. Ever. Has this happened before? Have you done this before?"

Rashid stares at Dad as if he doesn't recognize him. I almost feel sorry for him. I almost defend him, ready to say, no, he's been fine, but I can feel Adom cowering behind me, so I don't say anything. Dad looks ready to tear out Rashid's eyes if he comes one step closer to us. The driver stares at all of us, not knowing what to do.

We're frozen like that until Rashid blinks, shakes his head, and sputters an apology. He looks like a deflated balloon, with all the hot rage leaked out of him.

"I do not know what came over me," he murmurs. "I am sorry, deeply sorry. Please accept my sincere apologies. It must be the heat, the long hours of work . . ."

"I hope that's it," Dad says, firmly steering Rashid back into the jeep and motioning to the driver to get in as well. No one says a word all the way back to the hotel. It's the stiffest silence I've ever experienced, so brittle and thick, no one dares to break it.

When the three of us are alone in our room, we try to make sense of what happened.

"Rashid's not here, so I want you to tell the truth," Dad says. "Did he do anything remotely like that before? Did he try to hurt either of you?" Dad looks sick as he asks his last question. "Did he touch you—at all?"

Much as I dislike Rashid, I'm not going to lie.

Besides, I want to reassure Dad that we were fine without him.

"No, no, nothing like that!" I say. "He can be a little weird and he snapped at Adom once, the first time we went to Hapuseneb's tomb, but nothing like today. He never raised a hand to us, never."

Adom backs me up.

Naturally, Dad wants to find some kind of rational explanation. He suggests that Rashid is so involved with his dig that he's come to identify with Hapuseneb and that's why he took our comments so personally. But I remember his reaction the first time we went into the tomb, and I think it's more than that. There's some kind of connection between Rashid and Hapuseneb, and it's not just because the one man discovered the other's tomb. There's a reason Rashid found the burial place to begin with—he says he was led there, like I was led to the sphinx in the museum. And what about the ring? There's a reason Rashid took Hapuseneb's ring from his tomb and chose to wear it—it's not just a fashion statement. I suspect that Rashid has his own mystery to solve and it's somehow connected to mine. Reason has nothing to do with it—not with Rashid, and not with me.

21

The Bracelet

I'M READING BY THE DESK AND ADOM IS already in bed that night when the phone rings, waking him up. I answer it, thinking it must be Dad calling from his own room, but the voice on the other end is a stranger's.

"Meet me on the patio by the pool, the one with the fountain," a man demands in heavily accented English.

"Who are you? Why should I meet you?" I ask, my heart pounding furiously.

"Because you are searching for answers. I can give you what you seek," the voice cajoles. "Do not worry— you are safe as long as you wear the bracelet."

"What do you mean? Who are you?" I ask again, but the only answer is the sound of the dial tone.

"What was that about?" Adom asks sleepily.

"Nothing," I say as innocently as I can, already knowing I'll go. I'm too curious not to. If I were back home in New York, I'd ignore the strange voice as a prank caller. But here, after all that's happened, I can't do that. Anyway, it seems unlikely that a jokester would know about my bracelet. I slip into the bathroom and get dressed, hoping Adom will be asleep by the time I tiptoe out of the room. When I open the door, he's not only wide awake, he's dressed.

"I'm going with you," he says.

"What makes you think I'm going somewhere?" I protest.

"First of all, you changed into your clothes. That's a big hint. Second of all, I heard you say something about meeting someone. Third of all, I'm coming, too."

I open my mouth to argue with him, then change my mind. I don't have time for a big discussion. "Fine," I say instead. "But don't get in the way."

"In the way of what?"

"I don't know," I admit, "but whatever it is, I don't want you messing things up."

Adom's eyes flare. "I won't. I haven't before and I won't now!"

"Okay, okay, let's go," I say. I worry I'm leading both of us into a trap. Then I think I'm being ridiculously melodramatic. But there's no way to explain away the strangeness of this late-night meeting.

I can see light from under Dad's door, so I turn to Adom, putting my finger to my lips and tiptoeing past his room. Adom grins and hunches over, sneaking down the hall like a cartoon burglar. Once we get in the elevator, he puffs out his cheeks.

"Phew! That was close!" He laughs, slumping in pretend relief against the wall. I know he's teasing, but I don't think it's funny. I can't help feeling tense. But when we walk through the lobby, the night seems normal. A few businessmen are sitting in the café, talking in hushed tones. The man at the front desk nods to us in greeting the way he always does, as if it's perfectly ordinary to go out to the pool at 10 P.M. Maybe it is normal, I catch myself thinking. Maybe there will be a dozen guests, chatting and relaxing on the benches by the dark fountain. Of course there's no one else there, only us. And about a million mosquitoes.

"Who's supposed to be here?" Adom asks. "I don't see anyone."

I shake my head, slapping at my cheeks whenever I hear the high-pitched whine of a bug out to get me. Maybe it was a prank after all, somebody who thinks it's funny to watch people scratch madly at bug bites. Then I make out a shape on the bench on the other side of the fountain. I can't tell if the person is young or old, man or woman. Adom and I edge closer, straining to see who it is before they see us.

The figure stands up abruptly, looming into the light cast from the bar by the pool. Now I can see an older man with a sun-creased face wearing sandals and a dark galabeyah. I don't recognize him, but Adom does.

"You sold me the bracelet!" he says.

"Yes," the man nods. "I wanted to be sure." He stares at me intently, then nods again, satisfied. "Thank you. Now I can rest easy."

"Wait," I protest. "Be sure of what? What are you talking about?"

"You," he says. "I wanted to be sure you were the right one to wear the bracelet. When your brother walked into my shop, I recognized him right away. He looks like the descendant of a Servant of Hatshepsut, but he wasn't wearing the bracelet."

I look at the man's wrist. He's wearing the familiar

golden snake! "Do those people still exist?" I ask. "They're real?"

The man bows his head. "We have served the pharaoh for millennia and will do her bidding until the end of time."

"But you said something about Adom looking like a descendant of one of those Servants." I'm struggling to make the connection.

"Yes, the best, most trusted Servant, after, of course, his uncle, Senenmut."

"Meru!" I gasp.

The man smiles. "Ah, you know this name, too. Yes, Meru."

Adom is as stunned as I am. "So that's why I look like Meru? We're related to him?"

"And to more than just Meru. Only the right person could wear this bracelet, someone from a certain bloodline. When you came into the shop, I knew you had some kind of message for me, but I wasn't sure what until you told me you were looking for something special for your sister. Then I knew the sister was the one I was seeking. So, of course, I sold you the bracelet."

"What do you mean by the right person?" I ask.

The man points to my wrist. "It is a powerful charm, and only the right person can wear it. Anyone else would die from its strong magic."

I touch the bracelet carefully. "Die?" I feel queasy. Is the silver poisoned? Was there a lethal gas inside the locket that I released and breathed in, dooming myself to a slow, torturous death?

"Not you, of course," the man reassures me. "Because you are the rightful owner. For you, the bracelet is a protective charm. No harm can come to you as long as you wear it."

"How do you know I'm the right person? What do you mean?" I'm still asking questions. The more he tells me, the less I understand. I thought this man had promised me some answers.

"This bracelet came from the tomb of Thutmose III." The man pauses, as if for dramatic effect, like he's expecting a drumroll to emphasize the importance of what he's saying. Instead all we hear is the distant rumble of cars.

"Thutmose III?" Adom echoes. It's not exactly a swell of movie music, but Adom is clearly excited anyway. "Wasn't he the pharaoh after Hatshepsut? Wasn't he her stepson and her nephew, both at once?"

"Yes," the man confirms. "Thutmose III was a formidable warrior. His stepmother and aunt, the great Hatshepsut, trained him for military conquest, and he fulfilled his destiny. Just as you must fulfill yours."

"I don't know what you mean," I say, still staring at the bracelet, unable to grasp that it's almost 3,500 years old, that it comes from the tomb of a pharaoh intimately connected to Hatshepsut. I look up at the stars pricking the velvet sky. Those same stars were here when this bracelet was made.

"The bracelet can only be worn by a descendant of Thutmose III. That is how I knew it belonged to you," the man continues. "It will keep you safe and allow you to follow your path."

"I'm a descendant of Thutmose III?" There's a bitter taste in my mouth—he wasn't the ancestor I was hoping for.

"Mom was a descendant of Thutmose III? And Meru, both?" Adom sounds just as surprised.

"There is a reason you wear this bracelet," the merchant says, ignoring our questions. "You have a task to do, something left unfinished by Thutmose III that can be accomplished only by one of his descendants. His soul cannot rest until it is done. See, I am telling you what you wanted to know—why you have been chosen. And that you must act. You risk harming your ancestor's soul—and your own—if you do not. I cannot tell you more than that. We Servants do what the pharaoh bids us. It is not our fate to know more. We must be in the right place at the right time. Beyond that, it is not our task—it is yours."

"But the voice I hear is a woman's. I thought it was Hatshepsut who set me the task of finding Senenmut. Now you tell me it was Thutmose III." I wanted a connection to Hatshepsut, not to the man who defaced her monuments. "Does that mean I have to fix his damage, repair his mistakes for both their sakes?"

"I can tell you that Hatshepsut's desires were closely connected with Thutmose III's. He was her stepson, her nephew, almost her son-in-law. One who serves her serves also Thutmose III. I know this because when this bracelet came to me, I was told I could sell it only to a descendant of Thutmose III and that when the time came, I would know the right person."

"How did you get it? How was it safe for you to have?" I look at him closely. "Is it because you're a Servant of Hatshepsut? You're following Hatshepsut's orders? She's the one who wanted the bracelet to go to me? The old woman, the man at the hotel, the woman at the library—are they all Servants, too? They're all helping me do something for Hatshepsut?"

"There are many of us in the order, many who labor for the great Maatkare. Her power reaches beyond the tomb. She sets the world to right, spreads justice everywhere. She is *Maat*. From father to son, from mother to daughter, the bracelet is passed. This is my destiny." The man looks up, his eyes fierce and proud.

"But then why don't I have a golden snake bracelet?" Adom asks. "You said I was descended from Meru, one of the original Servants, but no one passed a bracelet on to me, just one to Talibah. It's not fair!"

The man shrugs. "That is a mystery I cannot answer. But looking at you, I know you must be descended from Meru. His image has been passed down to us Servants for thousands of years. Look, you can see for yourself." The man reaches into his galabeyah pocket and pulls out a rolled-up piece of papyrus. He unfurls it, revealing a beautiful ink drawing of a young man, someone who has my brother's ears, eyes, chin, and forehead—it's a complete copy of Adom, only older!

Adom still isn't satisfied. "Someone must have stolen my bracelet, the one that was supposed to be passed down to me."

"Maybe you don't want to be a Servant of Hatshepsut anyway," I say. "Sounds like a lot of work."

"But I am working for Hatshepsut—I'm helping you, aren't I?" Adom pouts.

"Yes, you have an important part in all this," the man agrees. "As important as your sister's, I think. And it is true that over the millennia, objects have been lost and stolen."

That reminds me of the bracelet on my own wrist.

"Actually, this bracelet was stolen from my father after my mother died. Do you know who stole it?"

"It was not stolen—it was taken so that it could be given to you at the proper time. It belonged with your mother, then with you, but not with your father. He is not a descendant of Thutmose III. He is not a Servant of Hatshepsut. It could not stay in his care. I was safeguarding it for you—not owning it—so I was not harmed. If I had tried to sell it to someone else or keep it for myself . . ." He trembles and his voice trails off, suggesting unspeakable horrors.

"The person who gave it to you," Adom breaks in, "was he also a Servant of Hatshepsut? What did he say about the bracelet, besides it belonging to a relative of Thutmose III?"

"Not a relative," the man corrects. "A direct descendant. And yes, he, too, wore the golden serpent. There are many of us, and our orders take us to faraway places. All he said was that the rightful wearer of the bracelet had a task to complete, something left unfinished by Thutmose III that had to be done before his *ka* could rest. And that the bracelet would help the descendant fulfill her destiny. I must warn you that generations have tried, and generations have failed. Whether you can achieve this task or not, the Servants of Hatshepsut will continue to serve the great pharaoh, hoping to find the one who will bring peace at last to the spirits of all three—Hatshepsut, Thutmose III, and Senenmut."

Oh no, I think, I was right—I needed to recarve Hatshepsut's name where Thutmose had erased it. Wasn't finding Senenmut enough? Did I have to clean up ancient graffiti?

"Can you give me a hint here?" I ask. "How am I supposed to know what to do?"

"Maybe you've already done it!" Adom jumps up and down with excitement. "You found the evidence for Senenmut's murder, you figured out who did it, and you brought the truth to Hatshepsut."

The man looks at me sharply. "Ah, so that is your destiny! No small task, I see." He nods, satisfied. "But that is as it should be. I knew much was at stake when I was told to take care of the bracelet. I knew whatever it was, it was important."

"But that can't be the task!" I protest, though part of me hopes Adom's right and I'm not responsible for the unerasing of Hatshepsut's name. "Why would Thutmose III care about Senenmut? Meru said the prince resented the architect."

"But Thutmose knew Senenmut mattered to his stepmother. Besides, maybe he thought finding Senenmut would make up for the way he trashed Hatshepsut's name and pictures on her temple," Adom insists.

I remember the falcon turning to me and saying, "Maatkare! She is here!" at the Red Chapel. Was that Thutmose's doing? Was he trying to prove that he hadn't destroyed his stepmother's soul? I look at my hand and feel again the searing pain that shot through me when I touched the defaced wall of Hatshepsut's temple. Maybe Thutmose III didn't kill his stepmother's soul since her name and image still exist in other places, but his destruction at her funerary temple was a savage wound. He hurt her and he knew it. Was he trying to make up for that? I wanted to believe Adom. It would make everything simpler, but the voice telling me to find Senenmut was definitely a woman's. Did that matter?

"Okay," I say, "I'm done then. I found the ring, I figured out Hapuseneb drowned Senenmut. Now when is someone going to do something for me, like tell me what my mother has to do with all this?"

The merchant looks up sharply. "Found what ring?"

I explain the whole story, from the old woman

giving me the small model of the temple to putting the ring back in Hapuseneb's tomb. I tell him about the dreams, the visions, the voice. It's a relief to have someone listen to me. It sounded far-fetched when I told Dad. But in the dark of the patio, with the cold stars above and strange flowers perfuming the air, talking to this leathery old man dressed in a flowing galabeyah, it all seems perfectly reasonable. It's as if I'm describing a family feud, not a four-thousand-year-old mystery. The man seems to think so, too. He strokes his beard thoughtfully.

"You have done well," he says at last. "And I see I am not the only Servant of the Pharaoh to help you on your journey. But the ring cannot stay in Hapuseneb's tomb. It is all that is left of Senenmut, the only home his *ka* can hope for. You cannot expect his soul to enter the tomb of his murderer!"

I feel a weight in the pit of my stomach. He's right, of course. But that means going back into that evil place, disobeying Dad, stealing, and then figuring out the right place for the ring. I sink onto the bench. Why do I have to do all of this? Suddenly, I'm furious at Mom. Why did she stick me with this impossible job? Why didn't she leave me some clues? Why didn't she do anything to help me? All she gave me was this stupid bracelet. I rub the scarab, as if I'm hoping some truth will escape it like a genie from a lamp.

"Wait!" I say. "What was inside the scarab? My dad said there was a paper in there, but now it's empty. You should give it back to me—it's rightfully mine!"

The man shrugs. "I never saw anything inside the compartment. I do not know what happened to it."

"What if it was something I needed to finish my task? What if the reason I needed the bracelet was because of what was inside of it?" I open up the scarab, showing there is nothing.

"I cannot answer that. But the bracelet itself is a powerful charm, as I have said before. It is a good thing for you to have it—of that I am sure." The man nods. He seems satisfied, even though I'm not.

"Yeah," Adom pipes up. "I bet Rashid would've strangled you today if it weren't for that bracelet. And you didn't drown in the Nile, so it's already protecting you."

"I will leave you now," the man says. "But do not forget the ring, if you care about Senenmut's *ka.*"

"But I have more questions!" I wail. "Please don't go!" Before I can ask anything else, he turns and melts into the darkness of the night. Adom and I are alone by the pool. The water in the fountain nearby splashes and the scent from the waxy white flowers swirls around us. The sweetness is sickening and I feel dizzy for a minute. I've found Senenmut, but I feel lost myself. I haven't helped him or Hatshepsut. I haven't done whatever it is I'm meant to do and until I figure it out, there will be four restless spirits—his, Hatshepsut's, Thutmose's, and my own.

The Key

YOU'D THINK ADOM WOULD BE TIRED, BUT he's bubbling with plans as we head back to the room. He's too excited to bother sneaking around, though he whispers until we're safely past Dad's now-dark room and into our own.

"I've got it," he says. "I've figured out what happened to the paper that was in your bracelet. Dad said something was written on it to help you with your search."

"So?" I ask.

"So!" Adom spreads his arms out triumphantly. "What about that small piece of paper you said the old woman stuck into Meru's book. I bet if you roll it up, it'll fit right into the scarab's compartment. And what does it tell you—Senenmut's name!"

Could Adom be right? I dig into my backpack, take out the silver book, and flip through the pages until I find the papyrus fragment. I roll it up and just as Adom predicted, it slots itself perfectly into the scarab.

"You did it! You figured it out!" I hug him tightly. "I can't believe it! Now we have all the pieces of the puzzle!"

"Right!" Adom nods. "We know what happened to Senenmut. We just have to heal his *ka*. We'll sneak into Hapuseneb's tomb tomorrow night, grab the ring back, and then we'll put it somewhere that Senenmut can visit, a place where his *ka* will feel safe and taken care of."

"Okay," I say. "There are only two problems with that—how do we get into the tomb and where do we put the ring? I know those are minor details to you, but they matter a lot to me."

Adom lies back on his bed. "Getting into the tomb is easy. We know how to find it and it isn't guarded."

"But it *is* locked. And a hotel key won't open it." I plop down on my own bed.

"Maybe not, but it looked like the kind of lock you could pick with scissors or a nail file. I've opened those kinds of locks before—I bet I could do it."

"Suddenly you know how to pick locks?" I shake my head. "You've been watching too many stupid thrillers or crime shows."

"I don't watch that kind of stuff! You need to believe in me more! I'm not just a stupid little kid."

"I didn't say you are. You've figured out a lot of difficult stuff. I'm impressed, really I am, but I don't know how to pick locks. I mean real ones, not those cheap toy ones that clasp diaries shut. Do you?"

"Well, do you have a better idea?"

"We could ask Rashid to take us back to the tomb one last time," I suggest.

"Like he'd say yes after how we insulted his beloved Hapuseneb." Adom glares at me.

I wince. He's right. The only way into the tomb is to break in. But can he really pick a lock? Maybe I should buy a lock cutter, the kind the school has to take locks off of lockers if kids forget and leave them on at the end of the year. I snort—as if there are hardware stores in Luxor where I could find a lock cutter! It's true, there are McDonald's all over the world, even in this small Egyptian town, but there aren't any Home Depots, at least not yet.

"Okay," I admit, "you're right. But maybe we should

practice on some locks before we cross the Nile, schlep halfway across the desert, and find ourselves at a tomb we can't break into."

"Fine with me." Adom grins. "So long as you give me credit for my great idea."

I pat him on the back. "Good thinking! Now I want to take a bath so I can relax enough to sleep. You should go to sleep yourself."

I turn on the tap in the tub and start to unzip my jeans when I hear a weird scuttling sound coming from behind the toilet. I stand still, listening, and the sound comes again, a light clicking noise. I inch toward the toilet. A flash of movement catches my eye and I hear the whispery clatter again. It's a scorpion, a big one, its tail arced over its body in an ugly, menacing way.

I stifle a scream and leap to the door, keeping my eye on the scorpion. I back out, slamming the door shut, and pull Adom out of bed.

"Come on, we're getting out of here!"

"But we just got back. What's going on?" Adom asks.

I knock on Dad's door, but the light's out and he doesn't hear me. When he travels, he often uses earplugs and takes pills because it's hard for him to sleep in strange beds. Once he's out, there's no way to wake him up.

Adom gapes at me. "What are you doing? We just tried *not* to make noise, *not* to attract Dad's attention, and now you're pounding on his door?"

"That was then, this is now," I say, racing down the stairs, pulling Adom after me, too impatient to wait for the elevator. I don't care that Adom's still in his pajamas or that my fly is unzipped. I rush to the front desk and tell the clerk there's a scorpion in our room. Adom listens, his mouth open. The man is apologetic, but not in a dramatic way. He acts as if a lightbulb burned out and needs changing or the towels are stained and unacceptable. As if it's a minor nuisance, not to worry, he'll send someone right up to take care of things.

"Does this happen often?" I ask. "Is it normal to have a scorpion in your room?"

"Of course not." The desk clerk is blandly reassuring. "It is highly unusual, and we are sorry for any inconvenience you may have been caused."

"Inconvenience!" Adom squeaks. "Someone's trying to kill us and you call it an inconvenience!"

The clerk smiles as if he's dealing with an unruly, unreasonable child. "No one is making an attempt on your life. This is nothing more than an unfortunate accident, one easily taken care of."

"Breaking a glass is an accident, spilling something is an accident. A scorpion is *not* an accident!" Adom is shrill. "It's not like we're camping out in the desert! We're on the third floor of a hotel!"

"Perhaps the young gentleman would like to step into the café for a nice cup of tea to calm his nerves?" The desk clerk hands me a chit. "Please accept a complimentary refreshment." He turns back to his computer, then looks up again. "Oh, and did you find the surprise your uncle left for you this evening?"

"Surprise? Uncle? What are you talking about?" I demand.

"Your uncle, the gentleman you've met in the dining room for most of your meals here. I'm sorry I've forgotten his name, but he asked if he could leave something in your room for you while you were out to dinner."

"Rashid!" I squeak.

The clerk smiles encouragingly, as if I'm a dimwit who's finally figured out something obvious—and in a way, I am. Rashid must have left the scorpion. Maybe he even arranged for the boat to drive so close to us. There's some kind of creepy connection between him and Hapuseneb's black soul. And the longer we're around him, the creepier and crazier he acts.

Adom gets it. He's staring at the clerk, his mouth wide open. He closes it and swallows loudly. "Yes, yes, we did—we found his little surprise. Thank you for helping him out."

"Come on, Adom." I nudge him. "Let's have something hot to drink."

I lead Adom to the café and we both order some herbal tea.

"It was Rashid!" I whisper.

Adom nods. "He really doesn't want us to help Senenmut. He'll do anything to stop us."

"It's hard to believe. He must just want to scare us. He couldn't seriously want to hurt us." I lace my fingers around the mug of tea, trying to warm the numbness out of them. I can't help it—I'm really scared now.

Adom looks shaken, too. "How do you know? You need to be careful! Promise me you'll be careful!" He grips my arm so tightly it hurts.

"Okay, already! I promise." I massage my wrist after he lets go. "And remember, I have the bracelet to protect me if all else fails."

The waiter slides a plastic tray on our table with the bill on it. I don't recognize him, but I'd know the bracelet he wears anywhere—it's the golden serpent.

"Hey," grouses Adom. "This was supposed to be free. This hotel is lousy. They let nutcases into our room and they charge us for stuff they're not supposed to."

I point to the waiter, but he's disappeared into the kitchen.

"Didn't you see the bracelet the waiter was wearing?" I ask. "He's a Servant of Hatshepsut, too! They're everywhere!" I pull the tray toward me and lift up the bill. Instead of listing how much I owe for the tea, there's a hieroglyphic. It's a cartouche, so I know right away it's a name, and it doesn't take me long to recognize it. It's the same as on the seal of the signet ring—it reads "Senenmut."

"Look," I say, passing it to Adom. "It's not a bill. It's a message. We're not done with this yet. We have to save Senenmut's soul."

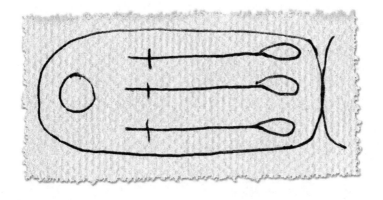

Adom takes the paper from me. "Senenmut," he reads. He has a good visual memory. "And that's not the only message. Look what else is on the tray."

A small key glints, the kind of key that fits a padlock, the kind of key that could open the lock on Hapuseneb's tomb. I feel a chill as I reach for it. Adom and I look at each other. Rashid or no Rashid, we know exactly what we have to do.

Back to the Tomb

ADOM WANTS TO LEAVE RIGHT AWAY, BUT
I'm not ready. I need to figure out how to cross
the Nile, how to get to the tomb, how to get back.

"Let's go!" Adom insists. "We can find some guy with
a boat at the dock and pay him to ferry us over. It'll be a
long hike to the tomb, but I remember the way—we've
been there twice now."

"But we need things," I protest.

"All we need is a flashlight. I've got one in my
backpack. Wait here and I'll be back with everything we
need." Adom pushes back his chair and jumps up.

"While you're at it, you might try changing into
some clothes," I suggest.

Adom looks down at his pajamas. "Oh yeah," he says, blushing.

"I'm coming with you, fearless hero," I say. "I have stuff I want to bring, too."

The desk clerk assures us that yes, the scorpion has been taken care of and yes, the room has been carefully examined for any other hazards. I'm not sure I believe him, but it doesn't really matter. We're not going to be there long, just enough time to grab some things and go.

While Adom gets dressed, I add a water bottle, flashlight, chocolate bar, and first-aid kit to my backpack. I'm not sure why I put in the small plastic box with disinfectant and Band-Aids, except it makes me feel more prepared. The chocolate will come in handy when Adom gets cranky during the hike to the tomb, and even though we'll be walking at night when the air is cool, it's foolish to go into the desert without water. With the carvings and Meru's book, the pack is pretty heavy now, but I don't want to leave the sculptures behind. I hesitate, then take out my sketchbook. I'm pretty sure no one would steal that. I tear out a few pages, fold them, and put them in my pocket. If I need to write down anything, I'm all set.

I put on my shoes and sweatshirt and scan the room to see if I've forgotten anything.

"Should I leave a note for Dad?" I ask.

"What for? We'll be back way before breakfast. He'll never know we went anywhere."

"I guess," I say. That's the plan, at least. I shut the door behind us and we head downstairs.

Once we're in the street, we stop to admire the full moon hanging high in the sky. We've picked the perfect night to break into a tomb. A few stars sparkle overhead, but the moonlight bathes everything in a silver glow, making the ordinary look magical. I remember how much I used to love Halloween. Not because of the candy, but because of the excitement of being outside at night, feeling the dark all around me, smelling the soft night air, somehow much gentler, less crisp than during the autumn day. The air doesn't taste like that here. After all, it's not fall, it's spring, and we're not in New York, but there's a different feel to the air now. A light breeze ruffles my hair, whispers against my cheeks. It smells like warm stone that's cooling, like sand, and from down the street, I catch a whiff of frying meat and toasting bread, someone's late-night supper.

Adom looks up at me. I can tell he's as excited as

I am. This feels like a real adventure. Like I'm doing something for once, instead of having surprises sprung on me. I'm in control, not just a pawn in some ancient game with rules I don't understand.

I take Adom's hand and swing it back and forth as we walk to the docks.

"If Dad finds out about this, you're toast, you know," I tease.

"So are you! Even worse—you're burnt-to-a-crisp toast because you're older. You're supposed to be the responsible one, the one in charge." He sticks out his tongue at me.

I smile. "You're right. I'm in charge. I'll take care of this my way."

It seemed like a good idea to find somebody to row us across the Nile, but all we see are boats tied to the piers—no men to pilot them. We keep walking, hoping to find someone. If we don't, I guess we'll have to borrow a boat, which is okay, so long as we put it back. That's what I tell myself, as I stop looking for a pilot and start looking for which boat would be easiest to take.

Adom jerks my hand and points ahead of us. "There! I see someone sitting on that crate. Let's ask him if he has a boat, and if he doesn't, if he knows anyone who does."

I follow Adom's finger. He's right. There's somebody, two somebodies, even, sitting on the dock ahead. As we get closer, we hear their voices murmuring and the slap of playing cards on the crate between them. There's enough moonlight so they don't even need a lantern.

"Excuse me," I say. "Do you understand English?" Both men nod, their eyes wary.

"Good." I sigh with relief. I'm not sure how I could have made myself understood if they didn't. Gestures can only take you so far in a conversation, especially when you want to be sure there are no misunderstandings. I don't want to get on a boat only to find us taken up the Nile all the way to Aswan!

I ask if either of them owns a boat and would be willing to take us across to the other side of the Nile and bring us back in a couple of hours. I unfold a crisp twenty-dollar bill to offer as payment.

The money makes everything clear, and both men leap up, pointing to a small boat nearby. One man reaches to take the money, but I shove it back in my pocket and shake my head.

"I'll pay you once we're back here, okay?" I don't want to be stranded on the western bank of the Nile, in the land of the dead. I want to be sure we can get home.

"You should have bargained with them," Adom hisses in my ear. "You're paying too much!"

I roll my eyes. "Who cares? This is too important to haggle over. Let's go!"

We follow the men into the boat. Maybe they're brothers or partners. Or maybe they just want to continue their card game while they wait for us on the west bank. I'd feel better if only one of them took us, because then I wouldn't worry about being kidnapped or robbed or whatever they could do if they decided to gang up against us, but I push down my fear, tell myself I'm being ridiculous. There's nothing to worry about. These are just ordinary guys eager to make some money, that's all.

As we pull away from the shore, I hear a splash farther down the river. It could be garbage thrown into the water. It could be another boat. I tell myself there's no reason to worry about Rashid for now. He thinks we're in bed with a scorpion in our room, right where he wants us to be.

Still, my heart is pounding as if we're being chased by crocodiles. Maybe the boatmen are planning on selling us into slavery and our new owners are fast approaching. Only there's nothing around us but water. And the men look like ordinary men, not sinister villains. I can tell Adom has the same worries. He watches every move the men make and doesn't relax until it's clear we're heading across the river, just like we asked.

It's funny, I think, how being in a foreign place makes you automatically more suspicious of people. Maybe it's because you don't know what to expect and you're not sure how to read people. Maybe it's the stress of not being able to communicate, not understanding what people are saying, so you imagine the worst. When the two men murmur to each other, I think they could be plotting to rob us and dump our bodies into the Nile, but if I could understand them, I'd probably discover they're simply talking about how one of them has a sick little boy at home, how the other is fighting with his wife again.

Anyway, I have the bracelet to protect me. And the Servants of Hatshepsut must be looking out for us or we wouldn't have been given the key to the padlock. Or Meru's book or the model of Hatshepsut's temple or the statue of Senenmut. I look up at the moon, thinking about how everything's connected—us to Mom, Mom to Meru and Thutmose III, all of us to Hatshepsut and Senenmut. It's been a long time since I pictured Mom, but I can see her clearly now. And I hear a voice, low and soft in my ear, singing a lullaby about the moon giving a baby silver kisses and rocking her to sleep. I know that voice and I know that song. It's Mom's. She used to sing me to sleep every night with that tune. I thought I'd forgotten her voice, but now I hear it again, as clear as ever, and I feel how much she loves me, how much she's always loved me. She didn't want to die and leave us. That was the worst part for her, not being here with Adom and me.

I stare at the moon and listen, feeling Mom's breath in my ear, the warmth of her body at my back, as if I'm nestling in her lap. When the song is over, I'm not sad. I feel like I've been given a gift that I'll always carry with me, a part of Mom that will always be alive inside of me. It's her love.

I look over at Adom. His eyes are closed and his lips curve in a gentle smile. I can see that he's been given the same gift. We've both been walking around with a jagged hole in our hearts, but now we're whole.

The boat bumps against the shore and one man jumps out to pull it up, while the other steadies the sides. I nudge Adom out first, then follow. I tell the men to wait for us. Since they haven't been paid yet, I'm confident they will.

"This way." Adom points and we start walking, the road a silver track before us. Neither of us says anything for a long time. We don't want to lose the echo of Mom's voice in our ears.

Finally Adom says, "I miss her."

I take his hand. "I know. I do, too."

"Do you think we're doing this for her? This whole thing with Senenmut, it comes from Mom. She's Thutmose's descendant. Are we helping her spirit somehow?"

I sigh. "I don't know. I hope so. Maybe once we take care of the ring and set Senenmut's spirit to rest, we'll find out about hers."

We walk a long way without another word. Once, I think I hear footsteps and that the boatmen are following us, but when I turn to look, there's nothing but sand and rocks stretching as far as I can see.

"What was that?" Adom asks.

"I don't know," I say. "I can't see anything."

"But you heard it, too," Adom insists.

I nod. "Either that, or we both imagined it. We've been pretty jumpy."

"Maybe it was a coyote or an owl, something that lives in the desert."

"Maybe," I agree, "though I don't know if there are coyotes or owls in Egypt."

"Well, some animals live here, whatever they are." Adom seems satisfied with his own explanation. I think the sound was more likely to be our nerves than a creature. I breathe slowly, trying to calm myself.

When we get to the Valley of the Nobles, the moon is much lower in the sky, but there's still light to see by. For a minute I'm not sure which path leads to Hapuseneb's tomb, but Adom seems to know the way, so I follow him. When the hairs on the back of my neck start to tingle, I know we're not far. The air grows darker and denser the closer we get. When the clean smell of the night air is clouded by a smoky sweetness, I know we're almost there.

Then I see it—the boarded-up entry, the padlocked chain fastening the crude boards used as doors. I turn the key and the padlock swings open. Adom and I exchange looks—we were right, we really were supposed to come. I thought I'd chosen what to do, but now I feel like I've been led here and I wonder if ghosts have been following us the whole way.

I must have said my thoughts out loud because Adom answers me. "We had to decide to come. It's still our choice. We could've stayed in the hotel."

"Well, the scorpion was a big deterrent, for one thing," I say. "For another, who wouldn't be curious about trying the key?"

"But we guessed it was the key to this lock," Adom insists. "We've made the right choices. We've been smart about this. Come on, give us some credit here!"

"Okay." I smile. "It was a brilliant deduction, my dear Watson. And now let's rescue the ring."

I pull out my flashlight and turn it on, pulling open the wooden board. Adom follows me, his own flashlight throwing out a beam. We haven't walked very far into the sloping corridor when the familiar nausea grips me. My head is pounding and my legs are stiff and leaden. I have to force myself to move forward through air that's as thick as Jell-O. Adom shines his light at my face.

"You don't look good," he whispers. "Maybe I should go by myself. You can wait outside, like last time."

"No," I gasp. "I have to do this. Me—not you."

I conjure up Mom's voice singing to me again, and my head clears a little, enough so that I can get all the way to the inner burial chamber.

"We made it!" I groan. I cling to the fading echoes of the lullaby, trying to fend off the smell of evil, as sharp as ever. The sarcophagus hulks in the center of the room, a pulsing dark heart. I can't take my eyes off of it. I almost expect the mummy to sit bolt upright, like it did in my dream, point a long bony finger at me, and curse me.

Adom rakes his light along the ground. "There it is!" he says. "It's right where I left it." He reaches down and scoops up the ring. "Now we can get out of this stinking place," he says, handing me Senenmut's last possession.

I close my hand around the thick gold band and right away my head clears and my stomach lightens.

"Hey," Adom says. "Look at this!" He picks up a stone figure from the pile of pots and sculptures on the floor. "She looks just like you."

I take the statuette from him and turn it slowly in the light. Although the face is stylized, it's clearly a portrait. I recognize the almond eyes, the full lips, and the slightly too-long nose. Adom's right—it's me. Why is there a statue of me in this tomb? Maybe it's not me—it could be Mom. Everyone says I look like her. But that still leaves the question, why her, why me, here?

I examine the figure more closely. On the chest, below an elaborately carved necklace, there's a name set off in a cartouche. I've seen it before, but I can't think where.

"Do you recognize this name?" I ask Adom, hoping his better memory for hieroglyphics will help.

Adom puzzles over the cartouche. "I recognize it, but I'm not sure where from—wait, I remember now! Let me see that statue of Senenmut that's in your backpack."

I shake my head. "That's not how you spell Senenmut's name."

"I know!" Adom's exasperated. "That's not who I mean. Just let me see!"

I shove the ring onto my thumb, unzip my backpack, and hand him the small black sculpture. He holds the two figures side by side, one white, one black, one light, one shadow. I take the loose sketchbook pages from my pocket and draw the statuettes while Adom examines them.

He nods and grins, handing both of the figures back to me.

"It's you. It's Mom." He pauses. "It's Neferure."

Of course! That's how Mom's connected; that's how we're all connected. I finally get it—Neferure is the center of the mystery, the core to it all. She loved all of them—Senenmut, Hatshepsut, and Thutmose III. She was supposed to reconcile them all, to hold them together, but instead her death tore them apart. With her gone and Senenmut's power weakened, Hapuseneb felt free to kill Senenmut. And without Neferure as his royal wife, Thutmose III felt insecure in his right to pass on the throne, forcing him to deface Hatshepsut's monuments to make his son seem like the legitimate royal heir.

I explain it all to Adom. "Do you get it?" I ask. "Neferure has to set things right, since it was her death that set everything wrong. Neferure is the one who's meant to do this. Hatshepsut's voice is calling to her and to me."

"I get that," Adom agrees. "But we're descendants of Thutmose III, according the story behind the bracelet. Thutmose never married Neferure. They didn't have children. So why do you and Mom look like her?"

"There's only one explanation," I say, figuring it out as I talk. "Neferure died too young. She had to come back and finish what she'd left undone, correct the problems her death created. So she was reborn—I don't know how many times, but always as a descendant of Thutmose. He was her cousin, after all, her closest relative, the nearest thing she had to her own descendants. That's why Mom and I look like her. We're related to both of them—Thutmose and Neferure. And to Hatshepsut and Senenmut, too. That's why when Neferure is called by Hatshepsut to find her father, I'm called. Part of her must be inside me. There's some spiritual connection." As soon as the words are out, I feel the weight of their truth. The ring pulses on my thumb.

"I get the relationship with Hatshepsut because she was Neferure's mother and Thutmose's aunt, but Senenmut didn't have any kids."

"Yes," I say, "he did. He had a daughter, Neferure."

Adom's brow wrinkles. "But he wasn't married to Hatshepsut."

"No," I agree. "He wasn't."

Adom's eyes widen. "Ooooooooooooooh!" He looks down at the statue of Senenmut cradling Neferure in his body, a type of sculpture Senenmut invented.

"Ooooooooh, you're right. It all fits." He traces Senenmut's profile with his finger. "And that's how we're connected to Meru, too. We're all related."

"And now I know where we need to put this ring. We need to bury it in Senenmut's grave, the one you found, the one that's directly under Hatshepsut's shrine."

"But the shrine is rubble now," Adom objects.

"It doesn't matter. It's still her spirit's holy place. There's still a link between it and Senenmut's tomb." I reach for the figurine of Senenmut. "Come on," I say, tucking it into my backpack. "Let's get out of here."

"What about the statuette of Neferure? Should we leave it here? It doesn't seem like she belongs in Hapuseneb's tomb, either. She shouldn't be a trophy for him." Adom offers me the sculpture.

I'm not sure what to do, but Adom's right—we have choices. We chose to take the key and use it. We chose to rescue the ring. And I choose to free Neferure, too. She belongs with her mother or father, not here, not with her father's murderer. I wrap up the figurine carefully and lay it in my backpack with the rest of her family. I don't have an image of Hatshepsut, but her temple stands in for her.

"Okay." I take a deep breath. "Now we can go."

"I do not think so!" a voice booms. A bright light blinds us from the corridor. I didn't hear any footsteps. Whoever it is snuck up on us. Could it be a guard? I reach into my pocket for the twenty-dollar bill, hoping a bribe will get us out of this mess.

"I'm sorry," I say. "We didn't mean to trespass."

"Yeah," Adom pipes in. "We're only kids having an adventure, kind of like Indiana Jones."

"Really?" the voice sneers. "Well, I would not want to deprive you of your little adventure. How would you like to spend the rest of eternity here, among the noble dead? Now that would be an adventure!"

"Uh, thanks for the offer, but we'd rather not," I say, trying to keep my voice steady. I take a step forward, holding out the money. "We're sorry to have bothered you. Here, take this for your trouble."

"It is no trouble at all. Before I go, I want you to know why you are being punished. I do not care about your pathetic attempt at theft." The man lowers the flashlight so its beam catches on the ring circling my thumb. "Especially such a loathsome artifact, the ring of a disgraced upstart. But I do care that you have defiled the name of a nobleman, that you have insulted the high priest and sullied his reputation. Such slander cannot be allowed to spread. So it will die right now, with you, here in this tomb."

"It's Rashid!" Adom yelps. He's right. I didn't recognize his booming shouts, but with the light lowered, I can see his face set in stony anger.

"You can't do this!" I yell. "You're a friend of Dad's. You're supposed to take care of us!"

"That responsibility is over now that your father has arrived. Which means I *can* do this. I am beholden to Hapuseneb, not to you or your family." Rashid sets down a basket, still holding the flashlight with the other hand. "I am offering you a lasting gift—to spend your final hours in a noble place with a noble spirit." He takes the lid off of the basket and tips it over. "Go!" he hisses, "in the name of Hapuseneb!" Something slithers out of the basket. Its coils are thick and when it rears its head, I see it's a cobra.

"Rashid, please!" Adom begs.

But the only answer is an ugly cackle as Rashid turns to leave. "Do not ask Rashid for anything," he calls over his shoulder. "You must ask Hapuseneb!"

I can hear Rashid's footsteps echo hollowly up the corridor and then a thud as the boards are chained shut. We're sealed in a tomb with a cobra. How can my bracelet protect us from this?

24

Snake Eyes

THE COBRA SWAYS BACK AND FORTH, HISSING at us, an evil black question mark caught in the beams of our flashlights. I have no idea how far a snake can reach to bite and I don't want to find out. I pull Adom behind the sarcophagus so that the big, black coffin stands between us and the cobra. Then I hoist him on top, safely out of range, I hope, and pull myself up after him.

"Okay," says Adom, shivering. "That's good. We're safe here for a while. But how do we get out? We can't stay here forever."

"I know," I say. "Any ideas?"

Adom stares at me. "I'm ten, remember? You're

supposed to take care of *me*, not the other way around!"

"Maybe this bracelet really does protect me, and I can walk right by that cobra carrying you piggyback."

"Do you really believe that one hundred percent, enough to bet our lives on? Besides, maybe that cobra has supernatural powers, too. After all, how did Rashid know we're here? Something creepy is going on."

"You mean besides being sealed in a tomb with a cobra?"

"You know what I mean!" Adom glares at me. "Didn't you notice how Rashid didn't sound like himself? I didn't recognize his voice at all, and I only knew it was him when he lowered his flashlight and I could see his face."

"Yeah, you're right about that," I admit, a bitter taste rising in the back of my throat. "I noticed that, too."

"And neither of us heard him walk into the tomb. We heard him leave, all right, but not come in."

I nod, swallowing down the sour fear. "I think he's connected to Hapuseneb the same way we are to Neferure, to Senenmut, and to Hatshepsut."

"And to Thutmose," adds Adom.

"After all, why would he care what we say about

Hapuseneb so much? It can't just be overwork, like Dad said." I sweep my light over the walls, searching for the image of the heart being weighed. "What if that vision I saw was real? What if Hapuseneb's *ka* was swallowed by a demon? It would have no resting place, so where would it go? Could it be haunting Rashid? Does he hear Hapuseneb's voice, the way I hear Hatshepsut's? Or maybe Hapuseneb chose to be reborn—into Rashid. Any human fate would be better than being devoured by spirits. Plus, Rashid discovered this tomb and wears Hapuseneb's ring—isn't that proof of a close connection?"

The light catches the scene, and once again I see Hapuseneb on one side of the scale with Anubis. On the other side a crane-headed god writes down the results. I wait for the image to come to life, for the scale to sink, the demon to leap, the soul to shriek in terror. But it stays still, the way a painting should.

Out of the corner of my eye, I see a flicker of movement, and I turn around, shining my light on the opposite wall where Hapuseneb stands by the Nile watching crocodiles swim. It's the scene of Senenmut's murder, but he's not painted there. I expect the picture to come to life, to show Senenmut tied hand and foot and thrown into the river, but there's no motion on the wall. I realize that whatever's moving is lower down and guide my beam until it hits the cobra. That's what's moving! Its coils flex and unflex as it slithers forward, closer to us.

Adom grips my arm. "What are we going to do?" he asks, his lips white with terror.

I think of the last time Adom saw a cobra, how much he wanted to hold it. But that was very different. He knew the snake was tame. What if this snake has also had its venom removed and we're terrified for no reason? I shake my head—it's not worth the risk. Besides, Rashid seemed serious about killing us. I don't think this is all an elaborate practical joke meant to scare us into singing Hapuseneb's praises.

If only we had some sort of weapon, something heavy enough to smash the cobra with. There are big rocks, statues, and vases all around us, but reaching any of them means getting off the sarcophagus, within striking distance for the snake. I should have grabbed something before we climbed up here, but I wasn't thinking. So now what?

The cobra has almost reached the sarcophagus, and I realize with horror that it's a big snake, long enough to rear up and reach our ankles. I push Adom behind me.

If it's going to bite, let it bite me first. Then maybe there won't be much poison left for Adom.

Adom clings to my backpack, almost tipping me off the stone coffin. "Don't pull!" I hiss. Then I realize— my backpack! It's heavy with the weight of the three stone sculptures—Hatshepsut's temple, Senenmut, and Neferure. I slip the bag off my shoulders and watch as the cobra slithers nearer. I don't want to move too soon. I have to wait until the snake is close enough, and it takes all my self-control to crouch there, waiting until I can get a good shot. As it uncoils, I see the hard sheen of the snake's eyes, the tongue flicking in and out of the leathery lips. Now! I take the backpack and swing it downward hard, hitting the snake in the head. It falls back, but it's still moving, still alive, so I heave the back-pack right on top of it.

I hear stone breaking and the cobra's tail twitches, then lies still. It's dead, crushed under the shattered statuettes.

"You broke them!" Adom sobs. "Those were magical gifts!"

"Yes, and they saved our lives," I say. "Come on, let's go." I jump off of the sarcophagus and lift Adom down next to me.

"What about Meru's book? It's in your backpack, too. Shouldn't we get it?" Adom asks.

I'm not eager to get that close to the cobra, but Adom's right—we can at least save the book. I take a step toward it and the backpack starts to smolder and smoke. Before I can come any nearer, it bursts into flames, engulfing the snake with it. The figures on the wall, so still before, start to shriek and writhe. Paint drips down to the floor, pools of color swirl around the sarcophagus.

I yank Adom into the corridor, trying to outrace the stream of reds, yellows, and blues that flows along the walls.

"What's happening?" yells Adom. "I'm scared!"

"Me, too," I pant.

Behind us the corridor billows with black, bitter smoke and a wail erupts, loud and anguished. It's coming from the sarcophagus—I recognize the scream from my nightmare about Hapuseneb cursing me. It's the shrill cry of despair.

We make it to the tomb entrance, but of course it's locked now from the outside. I shake the chain, hoping it's old and weak enough to snap. It isn't. If we were skinnier, we could squeeze out through the gap the chain leaves between the two boards, but we're much too big.

"Here, let me," says Adom. He takes the key out of my pocket and slips his slender wrist through the gap. I can't reach the lock, but his young boy's hand can. He fumbles for a long minute, finds the keyhole, and inserts the key. One twist and a yank, and the padlock opens. We push our way out, gasping for fresh air.

Outside, I hug Adom tight. "We're okay," I reassure him. "It's okay."

Black smoke boils out of the entrance. There's an enormous howl and the smoke is sucked back in, pulling the wooden boards, the chains, the heavy lock with it. The entire tomb caves in, collapsing on itself. There's a roar of rocks falling, a thick rain of dust, and then a heavy silence. I wipe my eyes clear of grit, and where the tomb once stood, there's now nothing. Not even a dip or seam in the ground to show where anything was. It looks like any other part of the desert. It's as if the demon has swallowed not only Hapuseneb's soul but his entire tomb. They've both been erased.

I'm shaking as I take Adom's hand. "Let's go home."

He nods, staring blankly, and we start to walk back the way we came.

There's no sign of Rashid. The moon has set and the sun is just beginning to rise. The sand is pink in the early morning light.

"Do you think the boat guys waited for us?" Adom asks.

I shrug. "Well, they haven't been paid yet."

"Yeah, but we said we'd be gone a couple of hours, not the whole night."

I stroke Adom's cheek. "I'm not going to worry about it. If they're not there, we'll wait for the first boatload of tourists. Come on—we survived a cobra, being sealed in a tomb, and almost being crushed by a rockslide. Anything after that is a piece of cake."

Adom grins, his face streaked with dust. "I guess so. But I wish you still had your backpack."

"I know," I say. "It's sad to lose those sculptures—and Meru's book. They were really magical."

"Actually, this time I was thinking of the chocolate," Adom says. "It sure would taste good about now."

25

Resting Places

WHEN WE GET TO THE NILE, I'M RELIEVED to see our boatmen silhouetted against the sunrise. They're patiently playing cards, just the way we first found them. I smile, thinking they're on Egyptian time. There's no hurry, no need to rush off. Just this moment, the here and now.

Adom tugs on my hand, grinning. "They waited!" He lets go and runs up to them, waving his arms and shouting, "Hello! Good morning! We're back! Thanks for waiting!"

The men look surprised by all the fuss. Without a word, I hand one of them the now-crumpled twenty-dollar bill. I trust them to get us back. We clamber into the boat and set off into the rising sun.

Now that we're not walking, I'm overwhelmed with exhaustion. It feels like we've been gone a long, long time. His head in my lap, Adom curls up and immediately falls asleep. My body feels like it's full of sand, but I can't close my eyes. I notice Senenmut's ring, still on my thumb. It's all I have left now of any of them. Even Meru's words are lost in smoke.

Except I've been given something in exchange. I don't have any proof other than my sketches, the bracelet on my wrist, and what the Servants of Hatshepsut have given me, but that's enough. Now I know the truth. I know who I am, who Mom was, and how we belong to this land. That's the greatest gift of all.

With the rhythmic splash of the oars providing the beat, I start humming Mom's lullaby. I hear her voice again. She's with me in a way she hasn't been since she died. Something's shifted inside of me, something that was closed has opened up. And just like that, I'm not tired anymore. I feel light and wide awake, even with Adom's heavy body slumped over mine.

The shore draws closer and the boat docks with a gentle bump into the pier. I shake Adom awake and he stumbles out of the boat. He's too tired to walk, so I carry him piggyback to the hotel. We're almost there when I notice a bird circling over our heads. It's a falcon—something I haven't seen around here before. It closes in on us, gliding low to the ground.

"Maat-ka-re," it calls. Then it's gone, disappearing into the rose-streaked sky.

Maatkare, I think. She is here. And she is. In Adom. In me.

I open the door to our hotel room just as the phone rings. I set Adom down on the bed and lift up the receiver, expecting to hear the old man again, the merchant who started all this last night. But it's Dad.

"Wake up, sleepyhead," he says. "I want to get an early start today. There's so much to see."

I tell Dad there's no way Adom's going to wake up soon. "He needs to sleep. Meet me for breakfast and I'll explain everything."

While I shower, a jumble of images flits around in my head—the carving of Neferure with my features, the swaying cobra, Rashid's face hard with hate, the paintings writhing and screaming as they bleed down the walls, the smoldering backpack, and the crush of rock as the tomb collapses. Over it all, I hear Mom's voice, the steady lilt of her song. Somehow she holds it all together, the confusion and loss, the love and loyalty. She's Neferure, the center of it all. And Neferure is part of me, too. The song is as soothing as the hot water coursing over my tired body. It's a quick shower, but I feel completely refreshed.

Dad and I talk for a long time that morning. I tell him everything that happened. I don't leave out any details. And for the first time since her death, we talk about Mom. Dad cries, but he doesn't close himself off. He lets the tears run down his cheeks and holds my hand, but he keeps on talking. He tells me how Mom and he first met, how passionate she was about her studies of the Eighteeth Dynasty, how happy she was at the births of her children, how much we meant to her, and then, when she was diagnosed with ovarian cancer, how calm she was.

"She wasn't surprised when the doctor told her," Dad says, "but she felt an enormous responsibility for something she hadn't finished. I thought she meant raising you." Dad takes both my hands and looks at me. "She did mean that, but there was something else as well, this task. Now I understand why she felt she was leaving you an extra burden—she said you would have to do what she had failed to do. It was your turn now."

"So Mom heard the same voice I did? She had the same dreams, the same vision? That's really weird." I shake my head.

"She must have, but she wasn't as clever as you at figuring out what needed to be done. I know she was given gifts to help her, the way you were. One of them was the bracelet you're wearing now."

I stroke the bracelet. It's good to know that we were both given this one thing. It's a connection to Mom as much as a clue in solving a mystery.

We let Adom sleep until noon. Dad reports Rashid to the police, expecting to face the usual Egyptian stalemate of paperwork and bureaucracy. Instead he's surprised to be told that Rashid was fished out of the Nile early in the morning. He was hard to identify because much of his body had been eaten by a crocodile, something almost unheard of these days. But he still wore an ancient seal ring, the seal of Hapuseneb, and that's how they knew who he was. I know crocodiles don't live for thousands of years, but I hope that the crocodile that killed him was at least descended from the one that devoured Senenmut. That would be justice—that would restore the balance of the universe, *Maat*.

We still have to figure out how to take care of Senenmut's ring. Dad makes a million phone calls. It takes all day, but he finally gets permission from the archeological authorities for us to put the ring where it belongs. Normally they would insist that the ring be put in a museum, but one official is particularly helpful and pushes the paperwork through. When Dad goes to pick up the permit and thank him, he notices the official is wearing a golden snake bracelet. The Servants of Hatshepsut really are everywhere!

That evening, Adom, Dad, and I board a boat and follow the setting sun across the Nile. This time there's a jeep and a driver waiting for us on the other side.

"And," says Adom, patting his backpack, "I have plenty of candy bars and water with me."

"This time you won't need them," Dad says.

"I don't know about that." Adom rips open the wrapper on a thick bar. "I always need chocolate."

We drive parallel to the Nile, then head inland, toward the Theban mountains, and pull into the parking lot in front of Hatshepsut's temple. Ours is the only car in the lot. It's too late for the usual tourist buses. The sun is low in the sky now and the temple is golden and pink in the dying light.

Adom finds the entrance to Senenmut's tomb first and we follow him down the ladder, using flashlights to guide us.

"Where exactly should we bury the ring?" he asks.

I pace slowly around the chamber, holding the small metal casket we bought to house the ring. "Here," I say when I come to the exact center, directly beneath the belly of Nut, the arching sky goddess. "Here is where he wants to be."

"Then let's start digging," Dad says, sinking a shovel into the packed-dirt floor. After fifteen minutes, he takes a break and I dig, then Adom. We want to make sure we bury the ring so deep, no one ever finds it. We're satisfied when the hole is deeper than Adom is tall. I drop the box down into the middle of the hole.

"It seems like we should say something, like a prayer, before we cover it up with dirt," Adom says.

Dad scratches his head. "What kind of prayer?"

"I don't know." Adom shrugs. "A prayer for the dead?"

"I know," I say, and I start to sing Mom's lullaby. We're putting Senenmut to rest for all eternity. At first there's just my wavery soprano, then Adom joins in with his own sweet voice, and so does Dad with his rich, low baritone. We hold hands around Senenmut's ring and sing him to sleep.

Filling the hole takes a lot less time than digging it, but the sun has set by the time we climb out of the tomb. I look toward Hatshepsut's temple, a gray-blue shadow in the dim light cast by the rising moon. I see it as it once was, graceful and whole, imposing and elegant. Above the central shrine on the uppermost tier, the holy place of Hatshepsut's soul where Senenmut's portraits were carved, a thin wisp of white smoke rises. A sense of peace washes through me and I smile. It's done. Senenmut's soul has joined his beloved's. They're together now in death, as they once were in life. They can rest now and so can their daughter, Neferure. So can Mom.

I take Adom's hand and Dad's and turn to face the Nile. It's time to leave behind the land of the dead and go back east, into the land of the living.

Author's Note

FOR THOSE READERS WONDERING HOW MUCH of this is true, this note is for you. The inspiration for this story came out of a family trip to Egypt. At the time, my children were ages five, nine, and thirteen. All the sites listed exist: the Cairo museum (currently being refurbished so it will be sleek and modern, not the dusty caverns described here); the temples of Karnak and Luxor, both large complexes of many temples and shrines built over thousands of years; and across the Nile from them, the Valley of the Nobles, the Valley of the Kings, the Valley of the Queens, and Deir El-Bahri, the monumental mortuary temple built for Hatshepsut, the only woman pharaoh, by Senenmut, her architect.

The books that Talibah finds in the library are all real, including the one she quotes from, *Daughters of Isis: Women of Ancient Egypt*, by Joyce Tyldesley. A paperback version was published by Penguin in 1995 and is still in print. The only one that is fiction is the translation of Meru's story. Meru's book was actually the earliest version of this one, when I wrote the story from his point of view. Many years and revisions later, the story is now Talibah's but incorporates fragments of my original drafts.

Hatshepsut, Senenmut, Neferure, Thutmose (I, II, and III), and Hapuseneb the vizier are actual historical people. As described in this book, Senenmut held an enormous amount of power for a commoner, and there are clues to an intriguing intimacy between him and the pharaoh: his second tomb, sited directly underneath the shrine to Hatshepsut; the portraits hidden in that shrine; and the use of a stone for his sarcophagus that was normally reserved only for those of royal blood. Moreover, in Senenmut's second tomb, the one where Talibah finds Adom admiring the earliest depiction of the stars in the sky, there are two inscriptions that strongly suggest the strength of the connection between Hatshepsut and Senenmut. One reads that Senenmut is

"Servant in the place of her heart who makes all pleasure for the Lord of the two lands." The two lands were the Upper and Lower Nile, and their lord, of course, was Hatshepsut. The other, tucked away in a dark corner, is the only image of Hatshepsut and Senenmut together. Their heads have been scraped away, the only damage evident in the tomb.

Despite Senenmut's importance to the pharaoh, he vanished from the historical record suddenly and mysteriously before Hatshepsut's death. Given all that, I couldn't help wondering what happened to Senenmut. It's the answer to that question that's the central mystery of this book, one I tried to resolve by imagining the court jealousies and power struggles that might have led to his abrupt disappearance. I was fascinated, too, by Senenmut's relationship with Neferure, portrayed on the walls of Deir El-Bahri in tender paintings of him teaching his young charge to hunt (a sport usually reserved for males), and in the unusual sculpture type that Senenmut created ostensibly to memorialize being tutor to the princess, but which implicitly presents a much more intimate and loving connection between the two, much more suggestive of father and daughter than teacher and student.

Meru is the only ancient character who is entirely invented, but the drawings he does are copies of actual works, including the fat queen of Punt, still visible on the walls of Hatshepsut's mortuary temple. All of Talibah's sketches are of existing works of art, beginning with Hatshepsut's temple and ending with copies of tomb paintings. The only invented objects are the scarab bracelet and the two rings, Senenmut's and Hapuseneb's, but the hieroglyphics on them represent their actual seals, and the styles of the jewelry are modeled on artifacts from the historical period.

For those in this country wishing to further explore Hatshepsut and Senenmut, the Metropolitan Museum of Art in New York houses several figures of the woman pharaoh, standing, seated, and kneeling; a Hatshepsut-faced sphinx like the one described in the Cairo museum; and the contents of the tombs of Senenmut's parents, rich grave furnishings that are another indication of their son's high status. Museums in Paris, London, and Berlin contain other objects and sculptures related to Hatshepsut, but the best place to get a sense of her and her commanding presence is at Deir El-Bahri, the mortuary temple that still holds and celebrates her spirit.

Talibah, Adom, their father, and Rashid are all

made-up characters, but the issue of how a family deals with the death of a parent is based on my own family's experience after the death of my husband. Like Talibah, my ten-year-old slipped a copy of the Book of the Dead into the coffin to make sure his father could find his way in the afterlife. I wish we all had such guidance in this world, but one thing's the same in both—knowing the names to call things, the right words for what's happening, helps tremendously. That's one reason I write books.

About the Author

MARISSA MOSS grew up in California and attended the University of California, Berkeley, and the California College of the Arts. She has written and illustrated more than forty children's books, including the popular *Amelia's Notebook* series. She lives in Berkeley with her family. Visit her Web site at www.marissamoss.com.

This book was designed by Maria T. Middleton and art directed by Chad W. Beckerman. The text is set in 12.5-point Bembo, an old-style typeface created in the late fifteenth century by the Italian punchcutter Francesco Griffo. The display type is P22 Acropolis Now and OPTIEve-Light.

The interior illustrations, drawn by the author using pen and ink, include re-creations of Egyptian hieroglyphics.